"*Enemies in the Orchard* is unflinching in its portrayal of loss and grief during wartime. Its narrative is surprising, its characters complex, and its focus on forgiveness and love, and the meaning of the good and full life, is honest and heady. Plan to read this in one sitting—that's how gripping this story is."

GARY D. SCHMIDT, Newbery Honor-winning author

"Beautifully crafted verse that moves the reader swiftly through a strong story, and a topic from our history that has much to say to us today. An exciting launch of a new author."

MARION DANE BAUER, Newbery Honor–winning author of *On My Honor*

"*Enemies in the Orchard* is a fast-paced, lyrical novel perfect for upper middle-grade readers that offers a new perspective into what it means to be an enemy and how we see and can also forgive others."

JENNI L. WALSH, author of *I Am Defiance*

"Dana VanderLugt's *Enemies in the Orchard* is a poignant peek at a buried piece of World War II history. This debut novel, rich in emotion, is centered around the universal story of friendship. I could not put it down. Readers, don't get too comfortable with the palpable setting and beautiful poetry, because this story is full of unexpected and gut-wrenching twists that will remind you there are no winners when it comes to war."

SKILA BROWN, author of *Caminar* and *To Stay Alive*

"A stellar example of utilizing point of view to great effect and the power of listening to new perspectives. A great classroom conversation starter on discerning what is true and seeing humans in a world often full of misinformation."

MEG EDEN KUYATT, author of *Good Different*

"*Enemies in the Orchard* is simply unputdownable. Rarely have I read a book that uses alternating points of view to such great effect. Claire and Karl are fully complex and compelling characters. The apple orchards are described in such detail, they become a character in and of themselves. As I read, I could see, smell, and taste apple butter, apple cider, apple pie. The story, based on the author's own family history, is meticulously researched, and the poetry is simply gorgeous. Full of vivid imagery, profound symbolism, and stunning metaphor, this magnificent historic novel in verse about a little-known aspect of World War II has the word 'award-winner' written all over it. It deserves as wide an audience as possible."

LESLÉA NEWMAN, author, *October Mourning: A Song for Matthew Shepard* and *Gittel's Journey: An Ellis Island Story*

"Seldom do we discover a book both timely and timeless. Dana VanderLugt's incomparable *Enemies in the Orchard* is not only such a work, but also evidence of the improbable—the formulation of friendship between those commonly perceived not only as incompatible but as given enemies. Thanks to VanderLugt's courageous heart and luminous writing, we will never forget the understanding forged across the ubiquity of hate by thirteen-year-old Claire and Karl, a young prisoner of war who reveals the inconceivable: a German soldier who holds a humane heart. We follow unexpected kindnesses, misunderstandings, and heartaches, while we daily walk and work with them. Timely? One has to be living in isolation not to recognize such. Timeless? How can kindness ever outwear its need? Based on a true story, VanderLugt's ability to combine exhausting research with an abundantly empathic imagination is astonishing. Be prepared to 'Never forget.'"

JACK RIDL, author of *Practicing to Walk Like a Heron*, co-recipient of the Best Poetry Book by *Foreword Reviews*, and *All At Once*, to be published in 2024

"The power of a novel in verse lies in its economy of words, a lyrical telling of a story distilled to its very essence, and Dana VanderLugt has done this masterfully. Told in two voices on opposing sides of the page—that of Claire, an impressionable, young teen girl working in her family's orchard on the home front, and that of Karl, a young German POW soldier forced to fight in a war he's not sure about—the novel covers a lesser-known aspect of WWII. *Enemies in the Orchard*, with its budding friendship amid the harsh realities and truths of war, is a story not only for middle-grade readers, but one for readers of all ages."

EDITH HEMINGWAY, author of *Road to Tater Hill* and *That Smudge of Smoke*

"Perfectly conjuring the time and place, *Enemies in the Orchard* is a stunning debut populated by characters who will stay with you forever. Claire, in particular, is the kind of endearing, complex character who will have you rooting for her until the last page. Written in mesmerizing and propulsive verse, this timely story will make readers think deeply about empathy, community, and the ways we are more similar than we are different, no matter where we are from. I loved every word."

SILAS HOUSE, coauthor of *Same Sun Here*

"A compelling and beautiful journey of history, truth, and courage, with connective and heart-stirring imagery, *Enemies in the Orchard* is a novel in verse that readers of all ages will hold in their hearts."

CHRIS BARON, author of *All of Me*, *The Magical Imperfect*, and *The Gray*

"Dana VanderLugt brings to life the human side of the Second World War as it played out in the lives of two young people in the orchard country of West Michigan. Imaginative, closely observed, timely, and hopeful."

GREGORY SUMNER, historian and author of *Michigan POW Camps in WWII*

DANA VANDERLUGT

A WORLD WAR 2 NOVEL IN VERSE

ENEMIES IN THE ORCHARD

BASED ON A TRUE STORY

 ZONDER**kidz**™

ZONDERKIDZ

Enemies in the Orchard
Copyright © 2023 by Dana VanderLugt

Requests for information should be addressed to:
Zonderkidz, *3900 Sparks Dr. SE, Grand Rapids, Michigan 49546*

ISBN 978-0-310-15571-3 (audio download)

Library of Congress Cataloging-in-Publication Data

Names: VanderLugt, Dana, 1979- author.
Title: Enemies in the orchard : a World War 2 novel in verse / Dana VanderLugt.
Description: Grand Rapids, Michigan : Zonderkidz, [2023] | Audience: Ages
    9 and up. | Summary: Based on a true story and told in alternating voices,
    follows the growing friendship between thirteen-year-old American Claire
    and Karl, a young German POW hired to work on her family's Michigan
    apple farm in October 1944.
Identifiers: LCCN 2023000451 (print) | LCCN 2023000452 (ebook) | ISBN
    9780310155775 (hardcover) | ISBN 9780310155706 (ebook)
Subjects: CYAC: Novels in verse. | Farm life—Fiction. | Friendship—Fiction.
    | Prisoners of war—Fiction. | Labor camps—Fiction. | World War,
    1939-1945--Fiction. | Michigan—Fiction. |
BISAC: JUVENILE FICTION / Stories in Verse (see also Poetry) | JUVENILE
    FICTION / Historical / United States / 20th Century | LCGFT: Novels in
    verse. | Historical fiction.
Classification: LCC PZ7.5.V365 En 2023 (print) | LCC PZ7.5.V365 (ebook) |
    DDC [Fic]—dc23
LC record available at https://lccn.loc.gov/2023000451
LC ebook record available at https://lccn.loc.gov/2023000452

Zondervan titles may be purchased in bulk for educational, business,
fundraising, or sales promotional use. For information, please email
SpecialMarkets@Zondervan.com.

Cover Design: Micah Kandros
Interior Design: Denise Froehlich

Printed in the United States of America

23 24 25 26 27 LBC 5 4 3 2 1

TO GRANDMA,
who always made room for
another chair at her table.

"Every war is a war against children."

Eglantyne Jebb, founder of Save the Children Humanitarian aid organization, 1919

Claire DeBoer

WHERE I'M FROM

———•———

APELDOORN, MICHIGAN

I am from hand-me-downs,
soft McIntosh apples simmered down to sauce,
and crisp, hard Cortlands eaten straight off the tree.
From the cold wind wiggling its way
into the second-story bedroom of our old farmhouse.
I'm from the perfume of the lilac bush
wandering into my window after a long winter
and the exhaust of Daddy's tractor puttering
away from our barn.

I'm from floors mopped on hands and knees,
and silent treatments louder than screaming matches.
From children should be seen and not heard
and young ladies don't act like that.
From why do you always have your nose in a book?
and idleness is a sin
and college isn't for families like ours
or girls like you.

I'm from the Lord's Prayer still recited in Dutch
and pigs in a blanket and pea soup.
From hard, wooden pews
and two Sunday services
(morning and night).
From dinner prayers that repeat the same refrain.

I'm from a mother born too soon,
kept alive in her mama's kitchen stove,
warmed by hope and coal
through February's long, dark nights.
From the cold, glass bottles of milk Daddy delivered
before he was hired to run our orchard.

I'm from two older siblings
who prefer me out of their way,
who remind me what I don't know,
what I'll learn eventually.
A sister already married and moved out,
a brother, enlisted, gone somewhere across the ocean,
carrying a gun, pretending he's not afraid.

I'm from the quiet whisper of another brother,
one I never met, a baby born fourteen months before me,
lungs not strong enough
to live through even one sunrise.
The empty space where his life should be
is a ghost, haunting Mama. His name marked
on a grave in the local cemetery,
but seldom said aloud.

I'm from a one-room schoolhouse
I outgrow a little more each day.
From diaries kept hidden under my bed
and tender dreams that bloom like apple blossoms,
soft flowers with the possibility of
becoming fruit
if they can find a place on the branch
with space to grow,
where the sun can reach.

Karl Hartmann

WOHER ICH KOMME:
WHERE I'M FROM

I am from smooth stones skipped
in the River Danube,
from Oma's lap, where she read me fairy tales.
From schnitzel, pork hammered thin and fried
in Mutti's heavy, black cast-iron pan
when Vati was alive and working,
and from weak stew,
sauerkraut with meat scraps, lard, and broad beans
when he wasn't.

I'm from work before play,
weeds plucked from the garden, wood chopped and hauled
before I'm allowed to venture off on my bike.
I'm from green forests and rolling hills,
summer afternoons building forts,
fishing, finding trouble.
Nighttime bonfires on riverbanks,
my friends' faces lit by laughter,
and scoldings for tiptoeing home too late.

I'm from eavesdropping
on conversations in the *Bierhalle*
at my Opa's elbows.

From the songs we belt out loudly
as we walked home,
hand in hand.

I'm from the tall brick walls of the *Ulmer Müenster*,
a church that took two hundred years to build,
a steeple that my great-great-great-great grandparents
strained their necks to admire, gazing high into the sky.
From rallies and parades through busy streets,
the same cobblestone I walked a thousand ordinary times
now filled to the brim with straight-legged,
saluting soldiers.
From promises of the rise of our Fatherland.

I'm from Vati's stern mouth
as he watched me, at ten years old,
fumble to button my new *Hitlerjugend*,
Hitler Youth uniform.
His nod as I slipped
a swastika band around my arm.
From promises two years later,
as he lay dying,
diphtheria stealing his breath,
to make him proud.

I'm from Mutti's worried eyes,
scared whispers when she thinks I'm sleeping.
From half-hearted jokes
that at least with all these daughters
she has fewer forced to fight,
fewer goodbyes to say.

I'm from three younger sisters
who resent my new role
as the man of the house,
ever on trial for their trust and respect.
From being born first
but still caught
in the middle. Torn between
honor and fear, conviction and doubt,
still a boy,
but expected to act like a man.

I'm from capture the flag,
slingshots aimed at squirrels,
and pellet guns pointed at birds.
Every toy and game and contest designed
to test my courage
and make certain I understand
that protecting my people,
protecting my family,
protecting my country,
protecting myself
means winning
at any cost.

I'm from a world
already arranged
for me, a destiny
already chosen.
A life of doubting
who I really am
because I've only ever done
just as I've been told.

250 GERMAN PRISONERS OF WAR TO BE HOUSED AT LAKEVIEW CAMP

MIDWEST GAZETTE   May 19, 1944

Lakeview Camp, west of Allegan, Michigan, will be a German prisoner of war labor camp, according to word received this week by A.D. Morley, county agent.

The camp has been conditioned for occupancy in preparation for 250 German prisoners who are expected to arrive in early September, along with an escort of 73 United States Army enlisted men and five officers.

Barbed wire fencing has been erected around the compound that comprises most of the camp, and Army-issued rations have been stocked in a supply room. The camp's barracks have been cleaned and aired, and a mess hall has been made ready for service. The army officers will be housed outside the compound.

The prisoners are being brought in under terms with the Federal Emergency Farm Labor Agency and will be lent out to area farmers in groups of six men or more to assist with the fall harvest. Farmers are urged to use every American worker before requesting prisoners be sent out.

Employers will pay the Department of Treasury the prevailing wage for services rendered, and from that POWs will be paid $0.80 a day, as well as given a small coupon redeemable at the camp's canteen. All prisoners will be guaranteed satisfactory and humane treatment as assured by the United States' participation in the 1929 Geneva Convention.

Claire

BUMPER CROP

●——————————●

I'm buttering toast and counting down
the days until school starts again
when Daddy pushes his egg-stained plate away
and leans back in his wooden chair
until he's balancing on its rear legs,
pulling on the straps of his denim overalls
with one hand and finishing his black coffee
with the other. When his cup is empty,
he pops up, drops it in the kitchen sink—
where Mama stands, her hands in suds,
her mind a thousand miles away.

It's been six months since my brother,
Danny,
left to fight;
a year since my sister,
Josie,
married and moved out.
The kitchen, the center of our house,
feels hollow with just the three of us.
The table, with chairs for eight,
stretches long and empty in the morning sunlight.

Daddy's sigh breaks the silence.
"Well, Claire-bug,

I've got one son across the ocean, fighting a war,
one hired man, Pete, too old
for war or climbing trees,
one daughter married and gone,
and you, thirteen years old and still in school.

You can help me with the math:
We've got two hundred acres of apple trees,
plus fifty-some acres of peaches, cherries, and plums,
a bumper crop.
That's sixty-five thousand bushels of fruit
for us to sell here at the farm or ship off."

His eyes are tired.
His usual optimism
hangs by a thread.

"What's a farmer to do
when he's got zero responses
to the Help Wanted sign
posted out front
and plenty of apples ripening up?
You think extra prayers for three months
of picking time before a cold, hard freeze
will be powerful enough
to keep our profit
from being left to rot on the trees?"

I give Daddy an "I don't know" shrug,
try to think of something worth the words,
but he's already squeezed my shoulder,
pulled on his muddy work boots,
and headed out the door to the barn.

Karl
KONVOI: CONVOY

●━━━━━━━━━━●

I've counted twenty-one days swaying on the Atlantic,
headed west to the United States.
There are hundreds of us
soldiers of the Third Reich,
now called POWs,
prisoners of war,
confined in this floating prison.

During the nights, I sleep restlessly
in a bunk reaching six men high. The weight
of the man above me so heavy
that even tossing and turning is impossible.

I'm the youngest
on this ship. Brought up the ranks to fight
because I can speak English.
Being a good student earned me
an early chance to die.

Barbed wire is welded across the portholes,
and nearly every half hour an alarm sounds
warning of submarines and air raids.
Over and over we are lined up on the deck
in life jackets,

turning our eyes to the sky
or staring into the endless water.

The captain says this ship zigzags
not to keep us sick and sorry,
but to save us
from ourselves.
Our greatest danger
is not the guns of the guards
who eye me suspiciously
or storms sent by an angry God,
but my own German brothers
in submarines,
aiming weapons straight at us,
trying to bury us deep
beneath the waves.

I remember the Bible story I was told as a child
about Jonah running away from God—
running away from his enemies—
and getting swallowed up by a big fish,
sitting for three days,
scared, miserable, and praying
in its hollow belly.
Then spit out onto dry land,
given the chance to redeem himself.

Claire

DUTY

●────────●

TUESDAY, SEPTEMBER 12, 1944

On the last day of summer vacation,
I'm not meeting up with friends or shopping
for new school clothes, but wiping sweat
below my ponytail, sticky
from the chore of cleaning
the salesroom 'til it's spick-and-span,
ready to be stocked full of apples.

It's too quiet.
Last fall, Danny was here,
working beside me, pointing out every mistake,
every bit of dust I missed,
each corner with cobwebs I was too short to reach.
Last fall, I would have done anything
to get him out of my hair, to leave me
alone to work
in peace.

Pearl Harbor was bombed
a month before he turned sixteen,
and I prayed every day the war would end
before he'd be old enough to join it.
This past January, he turned eighteen.
In February, he enlisted.

The bitter winter morning he left
feels as far away as he does.
We all woke before dawn,
a layer of fresh snow barely visible
through the inky dark.
Mama and I shivered
beside each other in the kitchen,
watching out the window as Daddy warmed up his truck,
its exhaust sputtering and sending up puffs of clouds
as he loaded Danny's bags. Still in my long nightdress,
my bare feet were cold on the wooden farmhouse floor.

Mama's voice and hands shook
as she kept smoothing out
the collar of Danny's army uniform.
Her hands reaching toward his face,
she restrained herself, asked questions instead:
"Did you get enough to eat?"
"Do you have the lunch I packed?"
"Did you double-check your bags?"

I wasn't sure if I wanted to bar the door
or stow away, if I was more worried
or jealous. No one in my family
had ever traveled farther than a few hours north
and Danny left to cross an ocean,
to go places so far away
it still dizzies my mind.

Goodbyes are awkward in a family
where things are known, but not said aloud
if they don't have to be,

things like *I love you* or *I'm sorry.*
That morning, we played the part
of a good American family,
and before Danny shut the door to leave
he reached for me, wrapped his arms around my back
just long enough that I can still feel the scratch
of his wool coat on my face.
"Be good, Claire Bear," he whispered.

I stop sweeping to wipe more sweat from my forehead,
still praying every day that this war will end,
that Danny will be home by Christmas,
that this will be the only fall we'll live
without him.

Karl
LADUNG: CARGO

The sun is just beginning to rise
as I wake to shouts of, "Land!"
and clamber up the steps,
crowd the ship deck,
stand with my *Kampfgrupp*,
my fighting group.
We began as fifty-five men and boys.
Today, twenty-nine of us remain.
Almost half were left behind,
buried on a battlefield.
We stick together.
Tied by where we've been,
what we've seen.

In the morning mist, New York Harbor
slowly takes shape on the horizon.
Tall buildings, standing whole,
pointing heavenward.
We glance at each other
squinting, surprised.
Our German officers assured us these landmarks
no longer existed,
promised us
the city was bombed to pieces.
That like our home country,

15

the United States
was smoldering and suffering.

I add this lie
to the others I've already collected,
unsure if it's seasickness
or unsettling doubt
that rots my belly.
A cold wind of uncertainty
propels our boat forward
toward a glistening American city.

Claire

RESOURCEFUL

●————————————●

Dropping an ear of half-eaten sweet corn on his plate,
Daddy licks his buttery fingers
and announces he's settled on a plan
to get the apples picked.

I pause mid-bite
as he pulls a wrinkled newspaper clipping
from his shirt pocket.
"This was published in May," he says,
unfolding the paper, its weathered edges proof
it has been studied several times over.
He summarizes its contents,
explains to us that a camp
for captured Germans,
prisoners of war,
has been built just fifteen miles away.
The county's Emergency Farm Labor office
will lend us a group of men,
just for the season,
just while we're short of help,
just until the war ends and boys like my brother
are back home to work.

Daddy talks fast, answering his own questions
before we can ask them,

like he may need the same convincing we do.
Convoys of American Liberty ships make their way
every week to Europe, loaded with supplies
to fight the war.
Why send those ships back empty?
Why not fill them to the brim
with captured German soldiers?
Why not use those prisoners to replace all the Americans
we've sent to fight in Europe?
Why not put our enemies to work?
How could we argue with common sense?

Mama looks uncertain.
Shudders and shakes her head.
"Saul, are you sure this is safe?"

I object too.
"What will Danny say
when he finds out
the guys he's shooting at,
the guys shooting at him,
are hanging around our farm?"

Daddy answers with another question.
"What does President Roosevelt tell us?
We all have to do our part.
Victory begins at home."

Karl
AUSBOOTEN: DISEMBARK

━━━━━━━━━━━━

TUESDAY, SEPTEMBER 12, 1944

The earth is uneven
as we walk down the gangplank,
our bodies still rocking.
Civilians stand near to ogle,
point and jeer
at the Nazis.

We do not grumble.
Just as we did not complain
when we were captured,
forced to set down our weapons,
march miles.
When we were transported,
sitting shoulder to shoulder,
tight against each other
on the cold, metal floor.
Relieved to feel the weight
and warmth
of someone else against us.

Since that afternoon in France
when the Americans surrounded us,
we have grown used to being
counted,
recounted,

searched,
tagged,
fingerprinted,
cataloged,
cursed out,
spit on.

I stand in line,
prepare to be searched again.
My pockets are empty.
The worn picture of Mutti and Vati
I used to carry was discovered
by an American guard
before I boarded his ship.
He held my parents in his own hands,
waved them in front of my face,
and then stuck them in his pocket.

As I move ahead in line,
I can still feel the breath of his laughter.
Wonder if he still carries
my parents' faces
with him now.
A souvenir from war.

Claire

KICKING AROUND

● ━━━━━━━━━━ ●

TUESDAY, SEPTEMBER 12, 1944

I can tell Mama wants to talk to Daddy alone
about bringing Germans right here
to our house on the orchard,
because as soon as I'm finished eating,
she brooms me out of the kitchen,
hands me a pail, and points to the garden.
"Gather up the rest of the green beans.
I'll be canning another batch tomorrow."

As I trudge the gravel path to the garden,
my feet discover a stone,
a misshapen, rust-colored rock
broken free from the hard-packed ground.
Slowly passing it from one foot to the other,
I kick the stone like I kick this news
around in my mind.

Once in the garden,
I drop my bucket and kneel in the dirt,
search for the green beans
camouflaged in the leaves.
I'm glad I'm allowed to wear jeans
and Danny's old leather boots
around the farm,
instead of the dresses and Mary Jane shoes

Mama forces me to wear
anytime I leave.

I look down to see a faded scuff on Danny's boot
and remember last summer.
The day the two of us raced along the train tracks.
Just as we heard an approaching whistle,
Danny's foot got caught under the rail.
I grabbed his hand and pulled him
to the safety of the ditch.
After the train rumbled past,
shaking the ground we sat on,
we retrieved his boot,
pulled off in the scuffle,
beat up
but salvageable.
I could see he was trying not to cry.

Rather than tease him about his almost-tears,
I kept my mouth shut
and tiptoed behind him into the bathroom,
avoiding Mama and her worried questions.
Helped wash the gravel
from Danny's cut knees and palms.
My hands steady
as his trembled.

Now I look around to make sure I'm alone
and then talk
to my brother.

"You think this is a good idea?" I say.
I can see him here,

across the row from me,
balancing on his haunches,
lifting up the vines, overgrown and tired at summer's end.

"I don't know," he says, not looking up.
"I know Dad needs the help, but I hate the thought
of Krauts walking on our land,
touching our trees,
coming close to our house."

I nod and agree.
"I thought we were supposed to hate
them, not give them jobs."

Before my imaginary brother can answer,
a squawking hawk flies overhead,
swoops into a nearby tree.
My privacy invaded by a bird,
I feel embarrassed,
too old to be playing pretend.

I put my head down
and get back to work.

Karl

DER REISENDE: THE TRAVELER

●————————————●

After medical exams,
showers, and delousing,
we are steered into a railyard.

An American soldier
walks down the line,
handing out knapsacks
that hold a bar of soap, a towel,
a toothbrush, and toothpaste.
I look up
and see my friend, Otto,
quickly wipe a tear from his eye,
embarrassed to find himself crying
over a the gift of a toothbrush.
"I remember when Mutti had to beg
me to wash up," I whisper,
urging him to crack a smile.

I dare to raise my head
and allow my eyes
to rise up from my boots,
the only part of my army uniform left.

Above us, armed guards
stand like statues

atop railcars,
trains that likely used to carry tourists
flooding into the city
to see the sights, have dinner, catch a show.
Now, the harbor bustles with captives.
A few Italian, most German
like me.

We murmur questions
while directed to file into railcars
from back to front.
Two men to each threadbare seat,
gray cushions once luxurious,
now worn more thin
with each month this war drags on.

After hours of standing shoulder to shoulder,
to sit is a small miracle.
Our eyes venture to shine a bit
of optimism across the aisle
and our necks turn front to back in wonder.

When the train is full,
the engine clears its old throat
and we start in a direction that must be west,
though no one has told us where we're going.

Porters enter the car to deliver
coffee, bread, and strawberry jam.
Soft bread and sweet, sticky red
explode in my mouth,
and I imagine I'm no longer a prisoner,
but a traveler on a cross-country expedition

aboard a train pointed in the direction of possibility.
Out the window, the world flashes by
and I forget that I'm still peering
through iron bars.

Claire
FIRST DAY OF SCHOOL

—————•—————

WEDNESDAY, SEPTEMBER 13, 1944

Germans, traveling halfway around the globe,
will soon invade Daddy's trees.

Today my feet walk
the same, worn dirt trail
to the one-room schoolhouse
on the corner.
The same route I've taken
every school morning
for eight years.
Other girls convince their parents
to let them quit school after eighth grade
or even before,
especially when there's a war on,
especially when their help is needed
at home.

I beg to stay.
Pray that I'll be able to finish this year,
and that next fall a yellow school bus
might pick me up each morning,
whisk me off
to a high school in the city.

For now, I'll settle for this same schoolhouse
if it means it will provide a path
to new roads,
to new worlds,
to my dream of becoming a nurse.

Karl
QUERFELDEIN:
CROSS-COUNTRY

As the train travels forward
and the miles stretch on,
we grow more incredulous
that a land could be so large,
that this much countryside
could belong to one country.
In the time it would take to travel
from Berlin to Paris,
we are not even to Chicago.

The towns we pass look flimsy, *schwach*, weak.
Wooden houses made of toothpicks.
Nothing like the solid brick and *Stein*
of home.

Some men sleep,
others play cards and exchange sad stories
of friends left dead and alone on the dry battlefield,
letters from pregnant wives that may never reach them,
families bombed out of their houses
by enemy planes.

I watch for signs,
keep a mental log of the places we pass,
the rivers we cross
on the way to a prisoner camp.
With each mile,
more aware that this journey
could be just a slower way
to die.

Claire

OVERGROWN

━━━━━━●━━━━━━

THURSDAY, SEPTEMBER 14, 1944

Twelve wooden desks face Miss VerWys, our teacher.
The kindergartners, Tommy and Gertie,
dangle feet that barely reach the dusty wooden floor
and count the minutes until we play kickball at recess.
I, the oldest, am all-time pitcher and umpire.

Miss VerWys has Margaret, Joe, and Ron—
the fourth and fifth graders—
up at her desk practicing multiplication
loud enough for Randy, Lori, Mark, and Linda—
the second and third graders—to catch on too.

Judy and Roger, both in seventh grade,
sit closest to me, pencils in hand, writing the same essay
on democracy and the American dream
assigned to me a year ago.

In the back corner, I maneuver my body
into my chair. My knees knock
my desk's underbelly.
My chest, no longer flat, seems out of place
in a room full of spindly legged children.

"Claire, would you mind reading aloud
to Tommy and Gertie?" Miss VerWys calls.

I sigh and set down my math book,
then move to the wiggling kindergartners
at the front of the room.
When I pick up the primer,
the page falls open to reveal
my uneven five-year-old autograph.
This book was mine
eight years ago.

I rub my fingers along that page,
remembering the excited little girl who sat
at this worn desk, grinning
and teetering
a pencil in her small fingers,
carefully pressing down letters one by one.

I look at the small faces
staring up at me,
waiting for help.
Their innocence stirs a memory
of the little girl I used to be,
and my stomach sinks.

The longer I stay
in this schoolhouse,
the longer I live in this town,
the more space
I take up
and the less
I feel I belong.

Karl

HERRENVOLK:
[NO TRANSLATION TO ENGLISH]

Closest definition: *master race*

●━━━━━━●

THURSDAY, SEPTEMBER 14, 1944

At dusk, we ride toward the sunset
and the train grows quiet but not still.
Like nervous chickens trapped in a pen,
we squirm and shift in our seats.

Since we were young,
we've been told
over and over
that we are special,
pure,
white,
clean.
Superior.
Überlegen.

Teetering between
homesickness and motion sickness,
my brain spins and fiddles
with the idea that perhaps
being in the enemy's grasp
is better than being in the battlefield:

dehydrated, empty-bellied,
meat for mosquitoes.

It is hard to feel *besondere*—
special—
after being captured
in the French countryside,
commanded and marched
forward by the enemy.
When orders were barked at us
while we scavenged for cigarette butts
in the mud.

It is hard to feel *ehrenwert*—
honorable—
when my fingers still shake
from pulling a trigger
that sent bullets barreling forward.
When in the silence
my heart still beats heavy,
reminding me
of what I took from other men,
other kids,
who wore the opposite colors.
Men and boys
I watched wail,
drop,
die.

It is hard to feel *sauber*—
clean—
when I can still feel the fleas

that buzzed around us
like we were dogs,
still taste the worms that fought
for their share of our food rations.
A shower may have washed away
the dirt and sweat,
but already I can smell my filth again,
the grime that seeps
into every inch of my pride.

It is hard to feel *treu*—
devoted—
ready to give up my life
for the *Führer*,
when everything I was promised,
the history lessons I was taught in school,
the duty and discipline
pounded into my head during military training,
the patriotic songs I was encouraged to sing,
grow fainter and fainter
with each turn of these train wheels
that crisscross serene American towns.

It's hard to imagine
ever again raising my arm
in a Nazi salute
as we slip past silent homes,
homes we were assured were burning
with death and destruction,
filth and fury,
when instead I see
windows glowing lightly

and smoke rising lazily from woodstoves that warm
well-fed families
sleeping safely in their beds.

The anthems of my Hitler Youth dissipate
and screams of the dominance of our German nation
are drowned out
by the overwhelming silence
of a wide sky
lit by stars
rather than bombs.

Claire

SUNDAY DINNER,
AFTER CHURCH

●━━━━━━━━━●

SUNDAY, SEPTEMBER 17, 1944

My sister, Josie, home for Sunday dinner,
makes sure her words are loud enough
to be heard at the kitchen sink,
where I am left to wash
pot roast, carrots, and potatoes
off the porcelain dishes
we're only allowed to use once a week.

She sways in the old wooden rocker,
legs crossed and eyes supervising me from the living room.
We may have just finished dessert,
but that does nothing to sweeten her bitter tongue.

"Is Claire really back in school this fall?
What else does she need to know?"
This is not a question
and she does not wait for a response.

"I quit school by her age and so did Danny.
Once this war is over and the boys come home,
she'll find a nice guy and get married.
Why waste her time

messing with math problems
and reading stories?"

Mama sets down her knitting needles long enough to sigh
and raise her eyebrows. "I know I could use her help
around here. But your daddy
still spoils her,
and agreed to let her stay in school another year."

My blood runs hot to my head,
and I'm formulating a smart response
as I leave the sink, hands dripping.
But before I stick my head into the other room
to shut up my sister,
Daddy pulls down the newspaper
he's holding in front of his face.
"Josie, you planning on being here
tomorrow morning at dawn to pick apples?"
His voice void of emotion,
he doesn't wait for her response.
"When I need help running my household
or handling my orchard
from either of my daughters,
I will ask."

I linger long enough in the living room doorway
to deliver a just-because-you're-older-
doesn't-mean-you-know-everything
glare to my bossy sister.
I may understand this conversation is finished,
but I am not certain if pride prevents Daddy
from resorting to asking his daughters to work,
or if Mama is right

and maybe he isn't ready
to force the baby of the family
to desert her childish dreams.

Karl
GEFANGENE: CAPTIVES

———•———

From Chicago,
we are transferred into trucks,
travel up a lakeshore
that sparkles long into a horizon,
like an ocean but without submarines
waiting to strike.

We pull down a gravel road
to a camp enclosed with double-barbed wire,
guarded by a tall tower.
Used to being barked at,
I don't blink
when an American officer bellows
for us to unload.

I was never given a choice
about the Hitler Youth.
It was a requirement,
mandatory for German children.
I was always afraid to voice any doubts
about my orders,
always afraid to question my duty,
my loyalty to Germany,
or our Führer.
Always afraid to admit

my skepticism
about the supposed superiority
of the Aryan race,
the catch in my throat when I was commanded
to name others
as inferior, parasitic, subhuman.

So when the American guards
show us a mess hall,
canteen, chapel, infirmary,
barracks with soft beds to sleep in . . .
when he gives us the rules
and then tells us we can wander freely,
my head is a muddle of guilt,
relief,
and surprise.

I can almost feel
the doctrine,
the certainty,
the loyalty
they attempted to pound into my head
since I was *jung*
trickle
out
a bit more
with each offer
of comfort,
food,
safety.

Trucks arrive all day,
dropping off loads

of captured *Deutsche* soldiers
until there's a sea of us
milling about,
a bundle of nerves and excitement.
We are assigned cabins
and work groups,
and lined up for vaccinations—
protection against whatever evil
still runs in our blood.

In another line, I am given a new name:
Prisoner G-5207.
I hold these numbers steady
in front of my chest
for a mug shot
and then am ushered
alone
into an office.

Two Americans sit waiting:
one whose stern face tells me he's in charge,
and one who knows *Deutsch*
and tells me, *"Platz nehmen"*—
"Take a seat."
I steady my breathing,
ignore the nerves swirling in my stomach.

"Are you willing to take orders
from American soldiers?"
"Ja."
"Now that you stand on American soil,
will you show respect to all
Americans, officers, and civilians?"

"*Ja.*"
"Will you set aside your allegiance to Hitler
in return for fair and humane treatment?"
"*Ja.*"
"Do you understand that threats or violence
toward your fellow comrades, American
officers, and civilians will not be tolerated?
"*Ja.*"
"You will be given lodging, food, and eighty cents per day
in exchange for your labor.
Do you understand?"
"*Ja.*"

Only one word required of me.
I am dismissed
to my bunkroom,
where I am left
unwatched
for the first time in weeks.

Because my English has earned me the unofficial role
of interpreter,
my fellow captives gather round
to confirm what they think they understand,
but haven't dared hope:
we may be better off as hostages
than heroes.

US ARMY GUIDELINES FOR INTERACTIONS WITH GERMAN PRISONERS OF WAR

Do not try to gain information
from a prisoner of war.

Do not talk to prisoners of war
except in the line of duty.

Do not ever believe a prisoner of
war likes you; he does not.

Do not think a prisoner of war will
not escape if he can. He will.

Claire

THEIR ARRIVAL

●━━━━━━●

I'm not sure what I expected.
Hard-looking men weighed down with chains?
Feeble, war-torn prisoners thin with despair?
Mechanical soldiers with hatred blazing in their eyes?

I watch from the front stoop
as a flatbed truck pulls into our driveway,
the back end weighed down
by a delivery of Germans.
Mama says we shouldn't be staring,
but stands close enough that I can feel her
warm breath against my back.

I count ten men,
the way I count deer when I spot them
gathered in a nearby field.

The guard is first out.
A rifle hangs loosely on his shoulder,
as if he has no intention of needing it.
He strolls to the rear of the truck,
yanks open the wooden tailgate, and
turns away, then pulls a cigarette out of his pocket,
bends to light it.

He doesn't look like someone who is worried
about anyone trying to run.

I expect to see handcuffs or shackles,
but the prisoners' arms and legs stretch
free as they climb out of the truck
and wait for directions.
Tall and lean,
cheeks ruddy, clean shaven,
shoulders trained to stand strong.
Most look closer to my age than my father's.
Several run their fingers through their hair,
attempting to slick it back
in place after their windy ride.
Three lean close together, whispering, grinning,
smiling like they have jokes saved up in their pockets.
One blond boy stands apart
from the rest of the group.
He bites his lip,
looking more nervous and shy
than fierce and brave.

Dressed in blue military fatigues
with the letters *PW*
stamped on their backs,
they raise their heads,
peer out into the trees,
glance around at the barns,
our house.

I can hear the low buzz of their mumblings,
words I know must be German.
It's a mean language

imitated by kids playing war in the schoolyard
with wooden guns and sticks,
or shouted by angry Nazis in the movies.
Even from here, their words sound harsh
and guttural, like the constant clearing of throats.

I've never spoken a word of German
but reckon it would feel like speaking
with a piece of hard candy in my mouth.

As Daddy moves from the barn to greet them,
Mama yanks my sleeve, urging me back into the house.
"Enough now, Claire," she scolds,
as if she wasn't right beside me.

I close the door behind us.

Karl

UNSERE ANKUNFT:
OUR ARRIVAL

●————————————●

The truck slows
and turns right.
A wooden sign in the shape of an apple
waves us into an orchard drive.
I shiver and cup my hands,
exhale warmth into my numb fingers.

The driveway forms a *T*.
A big barn towers at its top,
a work shed to the right,
a dirt road to the left.
From where we stand, the land rises before us.
Hectares and hectares of apple trees stretch
across the horizon.

A farmhouse, the owner's place,
flanks the driveway's right.
A woman and girl,
probably the farmer's wife and daughter,
stand on the front *Veranda*,
staring.
Both in skirts and cardigan sweaters
and nearly the same height,

the girl looks like a younger, slimmer
reflection of her mother,
who stands close behind her, on guard,
a kerchief covering her head
while the girl's golden hair, tied half up,
waves in the morning breeze.
Their arms are crossed at their chests.
I don't need to be close
to see the concern in their eyes.

My mind flashes to Mutti, my sisters,
knowing that the little girls I left
will be older, taller, harder
when
or if
I return.

Like the day I was captured,
I want to raise my arms,
show this woman and this girl
my empty hands.

Claire

WATCHING FROM
THE WINDOW

●————————●

MONDAY, SEPTEMBER 18, 1944

From the kitchen window,
I can freely stare.

I see the relaxed faces of the POWs
and try to picture them angry,
charging at American troops.
Try to imagine their curses
as they pointed their tanks,
dropped bombs from their warplanes,
aimed their artillery at our boys.

At my brother.

Under those prisoners' uniforms,
I make myself picture their hearts black with hatred.

I refuse to allow myself to imagine them
just captured,
hands surrendered in the air,
collapsed on their knees.
I refuse to allow myself to imagine
American guns pointed at their backs,

their pleas for their lives,
their cries for their mamas.

I remind myself:
they may look more like my brother than Hitler,
but they are still the enemy.

I remind myself:
no matter how harmless they may look
standing here on our land,
they have surely carried evil
across the ocean with them,
inside them.

Karl

DAS VORSTELLEN:
INTRODUCTIONS

●————————————————●

MONDAY, SEPTEMBER 18, 1944

Our guard, Nelson, whistles
and waves his finger in a circle
to gather us round
the apple boss.
Mr. DeBoer, or "Mr. D,"
takes off his cap and wrings it in his worn hands
as he speaks slowly and loudly,
like that is the key
to unlock his language.

"Names?" he asks,
and Nelson points to me,
whose English is best.
My heart beats
out of my chest
as I search for my voice.

"Wie heissen Sie?"
I point to my comrades,
then set the example:
"Ich heiße Karl."

One by one,
each does the same:
Otto,
Ernst,
Anton,
Heinz,
Friedrich,
Walter,
Wilhelm,
August,
Norbert.

The farmer nods and follows each voice
around the circle.
His eyes are discerning,
but his shoulders relax,
unbound from arrogance or ego.
Untrained to stand at attention.

I doubt his memory will hold each name
but I feel my chin lifting.
An introduction *ist besser*
than an interrogation.

"Jump in."
He jerks his thumb toward another truck,
one filled with wooden crates, ladders.
As we climb in, I glance behind me.
The woman and young girl have gone
back inside the house.

I wonder if they locked the door behind them.

Claire

RUMORS

MONDAY, SEPTEMBER 18, 1944

After reciting the Pledge of Allegiance,
Margaret, who is only a fourth grader but thinks
she knows everything,
raises a flitting hand.
"Miss, did you know that Nazis
are coming to work in Claire's orchard?
My dad told me all the apples are gonna be rotten
because Germans are picking them."

Giggles fill the schoolhouse.
Miss VerWys shushes and puts on her sternest expression.
I sit still, willing my face to hide its discomfort,
irritated that a nine-year-old's words are enough
to brew a storm inside me.

"Margaret, it's rude to talk about someone
when she's sitting right here.
Claire, could you explain to the children
what's happening at your farm?"

No.
I don't want to explain.
No.
I don't want to answer to a bunch of children.
No.

None of this was my idea.
No.
None of this is my responsibility.

I take a deep breath,
steady my voice
like an accomplice, not an opponent,
of this plan.

"The new workers at our orchard are German
prisoners. Soldiers captured by our troops.
They live in a camp
a couple of towns away.
Instead of putting them in prisons in Europe,
our president brought them here
so they can work for us."

The kids are all turned in their desks, staring,
listening. My face is red and I want to be done.
But I play my part
as the responsible, oldest student.
The trusting patriot.

"Since so many of our boys have been sent
overseas to fight, my dad doesn't have enough help
to pick our apples,
so the POWs are being put to work.
A guard comes along to watch them;
they're not dangerous."

Even as I say that last line,
I'm trying to convince myself.

"Thank you, Claire," Miss VerWys says.
She goes on to lecture, the kind of chiding
we all know by heart,
about supporting the war effort however we can:
sending our brothers and fathers
to fight, growing Victory Gardens, rationing,
extra prayers. Even doing your best in school.
"Speaking of which, it's time
to get started with our lessons."

Her voice strains and her smile is forced,
and I feel a flash of connection.
A few years ago, when I was one of the youngest students,
I saw Miss VerWys as unshakable,
a star,
old, wise, unreachable.
But somehow, my vision has changed.
She's probably only a decade older
than me. And not perfect,
but a master of the kind of pretending
that growing up
requires.

Karl
FARBAUSWAHL: COLOR PICKING

Mr. D pulls to a stop,
gathers us in a row of trees.
The September sun warms our backs
and the grass is wet with dew.

"McIntosh, boys,"
he instructs. "Color pick."
He paws through the tree closest to him
and plucks an example.
"Yes, sweet."
He examines a dusty, scarlet apple
flecked with specks of yellow,
rubs it quickly round on the chest of his flannel shirt,
and holds it high
so we can admire its shine.
Then he reaches to a branch
to pick another
growing in the shadows,
still mostly green.
"Not ripe. Sour."
He scrunches up his face,
puckers his mouth.

He waves the green apple toward us,
and tosses it at me.
"Try it."
I grab the apple from midair,
conditioned after months of going hungry
never to turn down an offer of food.
I crunch into the hard fruit.
My teeth have barely broken its surface
when I shiver,
force myself to chew
and swallow its bitterness.
I choke out a confirmation,
"*Ja, sauer.*"
The other men laugh.

Mr. D allows himself a smile
and then lobs the red fruit at me.
I trap it between my left hand and my chest
and he nods again,
urging me to compare.
I switch apples
and bring the red one to my mouth.
This time when I expose the white flesh,
it tastes like candy,
and I force myself to stop chewing
long enough to echo his teaching:
"*Gut. Reif.*"
Good.
Ready.

"Start with the best ones," he says.
"*Die Besten,*" I emphasize,
talking with my mouth full.

He nods at Nelson, our guard,
seeking assurance our assignment is understood,
then points to a few ladders in the truck bed.
Ernst and Anton move forward to grab them;
the rest of us string
picking sacks around our necks.

We begin two or three to a tree.
I try to be fast but smart,
make quick judgments
on what apples are red enough to pick.

Mr. D walks the rows,
monitoring, nodding approval
or shaking his head and pointing out fruit
better left on the branch to ripen.
When he stops by me,
he thanks me for my help
with the instructions,
then peeks into my picking sack
to see the apples I've chosen.
"Good, Karl."

Flattered he's remembered my name,
I find myself smiling,
caught off guard by how
different it sounds
spoken by this Michigan farmer.

He smiles back and I almost expect him
to clap my back in encouragement,
but he keeps a safe distance.

Claire

TRAITOR

●━━━━━●

My schoolbag still heavy on my shoulder,
Mama greets me in the entryway
with a basket of wash to hang on the line.
From the backyard,
I can see Daddy return from the field
on the tractor.
The new men, here for their second day,
sit on the back of the trailer
as it comes up the hill from the trees.
They perch on the edges of crates
filled with freshly picked McIntosh.
They laugh and smile,
wearing only white undershirts,
their prisoner uniforms stripped off
in the warm sun.
One bites into an apple.

They're enjoying the ride
like they belong here, like this is theirs.
Like they're not the enemy.

Daddy shows them to the grader,
where we clean and sort.
Toss out the bad apples,
separate the bruised fruit,

determine the Firsts—
the largest and flawless fruit—
and the Seconds—
apples too small, green, or blemished
to sell at full price.

I pull wet sheets from the basket
and throw them over the clothesline,
glad the fabric blocks my view.

These men have each played a part
in tearing our world apart,
and now they make themselves at home
in our land,
touch our trees,
pick our fruit.
Even from here, I can see Dad's nod,
his assuring grin
as he works beside them, training them.

Like there are wasps buzzing in my head,
I try to make sense
of how he has so easily given these strangers
the right to be here
in the shelter
of our trees.

Karl
DIE EINWEIHUNG: INITIATION

●━━━━━━━━●

Back at camp
after a second day of picking,
we line up for dinner.
There are more than two hundred of us
crowding a mess hall,
boys and men,
each assigned to a different farm or factory.
We look like kids at summer camp,
except for the blue uniforms with *PW*
stamped on our backs,
and the double-barbed wire that
lines the perimeter of the grounds.

This is not the daring soldier's life
I was promised.

At ten years old
I stood, shoulders back,
head up,
in a straight line next to my friends.
Told to raise my right hand,
told it was a holy hour,
told that millions of other young Germans—
proud young men
like me—

were raising their hands
at the exact same moment.
Told I was lucky,
chosen,
to be part of the *Jungvolk*,
the Hitler Youth.

If I didn't think too hard
or ask too many questions,
it was easy.

Easy to join the games,
the marching, the singing,
the playing.
Easy to sit around a campfire
and cheer stories of my country's heroic past.

Easy to put my faith
in our smiling Führer, Adolf Hitler.
Who loved his dog, Blondi,
a German shepherd,
just like I loved my dog.
Who gently leaned over,
accepting bouquets of flowers from little girls
who looked like my sisters.
Adolf Hitler, whose
"stature reaches the very stars,"
but deep down,
"Er ist genau wie du and ich."
He is just like you and me.

I am handed my plate—
green beans, potatoes,

a brown piece of meat—
then head to a wooden table
to eat elbow to elbow
with my fellow comrades,
companions,
captives.

As I pick up my fork,
it occurs to me
that for all the stories fed to me,
all the promises made to me,
all the vows I was forced to take
by the Reich,
it's now,
as a captive,
that I'm more at peace
than I ever was
fighting at home.

Claire

DOING THE MATH

●━━━━━●
WEDNESDAY, SEPTEMBER 20, 1944

At my desk at the back of the schoolhouse,
I attempt to focus on my algebra,
but try as a I might,
even two days later
I can still hear Margaret's voice in my head,
her warning about the dangerous Germans
my family is allowing in our trees.

I know she's only an echo
of what the rest of the town is whispering.
What the neighbors talk about
when they see each other at the market.
What our friends say
when we're out of earshot.

And though my head spun
yesterday at the sight of the men
on our farm,
a small part of me also understands
that hiring these German workers
allows me
to stay in school.

My uncertainty and questions
seesaw with relief.

Relief that Daddy has found workers—
whoever they are
and however they're acquired—
and that if they're in the orchard,
I don't have to be.
Relief that welcoming Germans—
men who only days before
would have willingly shot at my brother—
relieves me
of responsibility.

Like Daddy who hired them,
like the president who shipped them over an ocean,
I justify my feelings
as simple math.
Because when these POWs are picking our apples,
they're also giving me an answer
to the problem
I've been trying to solve.

Karl

HINTER DEM STACHELDRAHT:
BEHIND THE BARBED WIRE

WEDNESDAY, SEPTEMBER 20, 1944

Nelson assures us
that the United States War Department
weeded out
the worst of us,
would never allow real Nazis
to work and wander
civilian fields and orchards.

They would never allow someone to live in the camp
who really believes
the world could be saved
with German domination,
someone who actually believes
the Aryan race is superior
to all others.

They would never allow someone
so thick with hate,
so deep in conviction,
so completely devoted to Hitler
that he would hold his ideals
higher than the chance to surrender.
Higher than the promise of safety,

                    sustenance,
                        peace.

                They say this camp is clean and secure,
                    a carefully run operation.

                        But when the guards
                        turn their backs,
                        exit the room,
                        leave us alone,
                            the truth
                            trickles
                            out.

Claire

FRIDAY NIGHT PICTURE SHOW

●————————————————————●

FRIDAY, SEPTEMBER 22, 1944

Half the town has sacrificed the cool breeze
of a perfect September evening
to squeeze into this dark, humid town hall,
a rectangle box of a building that plays the part
of a boardroom, basketball court, or banquet hall
depending on the night.
An old projector waits
to spin a film reel through its gears,
clicking like the sound of steady rain on a rooftop.

Mrs. Cornelius, who plays the solemn church organ,
bangs a ragtime tune on a piano
as people mill in,
stop to socialize as they find seats.
The adults sit in back,
the youngest kids swarm up front on the floor.
I've graduated to the first row
of hard, wooden folding chairs.

I settle in between two old classmates:
Sara, a sort-of friend who chatters too much,
and Jordan, the once-freckled little boy
who teased me in Sunday school
and now taps his sneaker nervously on the wooden floor.

Neither came back to school this fall
for eighth grade.

I cross one leg over the other
even though it feels uncomfortable,
tug my plaid skirt over my bare legs,
worried my white socks make me look like a little girl.
I should be wearing stockings,
but the government is rationing them.
Nylon is needed for parachutes.

We eat buttery popcorn,
our greasy fingers ready to clap
when the heroes stand up to the Nazis.
The little kids jump up when the good guys win,
cheer when the German planes are shot down,
when the enemy soldiers are eliminated one by one.

Behind me are empty seats
where my brother and his friends should be sitting.
It's easier if I don't let myself think of Danny
as one of the soldiers being shot at.
One of the heroes going down.
Easier if I don't think of the POWs in our orchard
as the Germans on the other sides of the guns.

My older sister, Josie, whose husband is overseas,
sits with the other war wives. Sally is next to her,
bouncing a round-faced toddler on her lap;
Martha on the other side, cradling
her rounded, pregnant belly,
a goodbye baby whose birth will be announced
to his daddy through V-mail.

The girls, playing a new role as wives,
watch the screen with hope,
smiling and pretending
that every story ends
with happily
ever after.

Karl
IN DER KASERNE:
IN THE BARRACKS

●━━━━━━━●

FRIDAY, SEPTEMBER 22, 1944

Thirty bunk beds.
Coarse army blankets
and one woodstove.
Shelves and lockers
stocked with westerns, mysteries,
cards for gambling.
Bubble gum, gumdrops,
cigarettes bought with our weekly allowance
at the camp canteen.

Hanging above the beds:
tattered pictures
of wives, girlfriends,
babies born since we've been away,
brothers, sisters, fathers, mothers.
Pinups of girls with long legs,
sly smiles,
torn from magazines.

Under my pillow are letters
half-written,
waiting to be finished and sent home,
stored beside those received

from Mutti and my sisters.
Pages thin from being carried
in pockets, read and refolded.

I keep my belongings hidden
better than others.
Loyalists like Ernst, Heinz, and Anton
make sure the rest of us,
those they consider traitors,
notice
the swastikas
they've carved with pocketknives
on the inside of their wooden bedposts,
tucked away from the eyes of the guards.
They make sure we notice
their solemn salutes
and hear their mutterings
of *Sieg Heil*
each morning
when the camp's American flag is raised.

These are the men we avoid
after sunset,
when the lights go out,
when no one is there to see
a hard jab in the side
or to overhear a whispered threat.

This cabin may look like a home
to an average group of campers,
but look closer
and you'll see new lines drawn,
new battlefields defined

between Hitler's true believers
and those of us with the courage
to lose our faith.

Claire

LUNCH BREAK

——●————————————●——

MONDAY, SEPTEMBER 25, 1944

I can smell chili simmering on the stove
and cornbread baking in the oven
as I walk in the door for lunch.
Mama shakes her head.
"Daddy says that anyone who works
at his farm needs more than the hard bread
and summer sausage the camp sends.
I've given up arguing.
What are a few more mouths to feed?"

From the back window I turn to see
~~soldiers~~
~~boys~~
enemies
gathered in my backyard.
Half sit on the wooden benches of our picnic table;
one leans, legs stretched out like a ladder, against its end;
two sit, back ends on the ground, against the red maple;
two others sprawl on their backs in the grass,
eyes to the sky.
Nelson, the guard who doesn't do much guarding,
wanders around the yard
looking into barns,
being nosy.

"Your daddy dropped them off,
then headed back out to the trees
to see about a stalled tractor." Mama sighs.
"You may as well help me, Claire."

"You want me to go out there" I ask,
"like some kind of waitress?
Hey, fellas! I know you usually try to shoot Americans,
but I come in peace
with chili and cornbread."

"Claire." Mama points at me with her ladle.
"Quit being dramatic.
Your father says they're good workers,
just boys caught up
in something bigger than themselves."

"Just innocent boys
raised by Hitler," I counter.
I see doubt buried in her eyes,
but she dismisses me
with a warning and logic.

"If Danny was captured
and left in the care of a German family,
I sure hope they'd feed him."

She hands me a pitcher of lemonade
and a stack of bowls, spoons balancing inside.
"Go on. I'll be right behind you."
She nods to the door.

The ground is uneven and I guide myself
to the far side of the table.
I keep my eyes on the teetering bowls.

Chatter floats lightly
on the September breeze.
Are these German words I don't understand
about me?

The POWs grow silent
as I set down the lemonade
and bowls hurriedly.
I don't look up to see
whether they smirk or smile.

Before I can turn to leave,
a sandy blond
~~boy~~
~~soldier~~
enemy
puts a hand to his chest and says,
"*Karl.*
Danke."

The friendliness on his face
and the quietness in his eyes
surprises me.
I register how close
he is to my own age.
Like someone I might talk to
at school, at church, in town.

He probably assumes
that my quick nod in return
means I think it's wise to
keep my distance.

He is right.

Karl
MITTAGSPAUSE: LUNCH BREAK

Mr. DeBoer drops off the ten of us
at a picnic table next to his house
for lunch. Says our hard work
has earned us a decent meal.
No one argues with that.

We're lazing around,
wondering what's on the menu,
when the farmer's daughter
comes out carrying dishes
and a pitcher of lemonade.
She wears a ponytail
and a serious expression,
her mouth drawn taut.

Her mom follows a few steps behind her
with a steaming pot.
"Claire, make room on the table
for me to put this down."

I thank Claire.
She seems surprised,
but doesn't say anything.

I guess I don't blame her.

How is she to know
that the orders I've been given
to fight,
to threaten,
to hate
feel as faraway as my hometown?

Convincing an American girl
that I'm not dangerous
will take more
than a smile and a *danke*.

Claire

RECESS ATTACK

●━━━━━●

Dismissed for recess, the youngest kids
are bounding down the schoolhouse steps
when I hear Joe yell, "Look! Germans!"

I cringe and join the others
gathered round and pointing
at our POWs, who pick apples in the trees
that border the schoolyard.

Too old and responsible
to join in their shenanigans
and too embarrassed
to answer more questions,
I turn my head,
start toward a tree with a book,
hoping to avoid explaining again
to a bunch of kids
why my daddy is letting Nazis
pick our fruit.

It doesn't take long until the boys are off,
retrieving marbles stored away in their lunchboxes
and slingshots stowed away in their bags
to begin an all-out assault.

"This is for our brothers!"
they scream, aiming for the soldiers,
who drop their picking sacks and crates
to dodge and duck the incoming missiles.

The Germans smile and chuckle,
decide to take up their expected role
in this harmless war.
I watch as they bend and scramble,
search for the fallen
marbles in the weeds
or catch them in midair,
prepare to return fire.

Without any sense of urgency,
Nelson, their guard, lifts himself from the trailer
where he was lounging,
raises his hands to direct his workers
to drop their weapons, return to work,
then strolls our way. With little attempt
to disguise his grin, he delivers the schoolyard assailants
a mild scolding.
The kind of boys-will-be-boys tone
that resembles more of a pat on the head
than a paddle on the bottom.

At the same time, Miss VerWys
runs from the schoolhouse
to investigate the commotion,
looking much less amused than Nelson.
She wags her finger with one hand
and rings her bell with the other.

Recess comes to an early end.

I stand, brush dust off my skirt
like I attempt to dust off the mess of emotions
that swirl in my muddled mind.
Part of me wants to scream out,
to let everyone know that these Germans
have nothing to do with me,
but then I hear the echo of my mom's words,
her question about how I'd want Danny treated
if he were a prisoner
in an enemy's small town.

As I pass, I dare a quick glance
out into the trees. Karl is
balanced up on a ladder,
brushing his shaggy hair out of his eyes.
He nods my way and then raises his hand
in a tentative wave.

I look away,
pick up my pace,
pretend not to notice him.
More worried about being called a traitor
than willing to defend my doubts,
than willing to take the risk
of being kind.

Karl

BADEHAUS: BATHHOUSE

---●———————●---

TUESDAY, SEPTEMBER 26, 1944

After a full day of work
and a game of soccer in the yard,
I need a shower.
The water is lukewarm.
I rush to get clean.

I turn off the faucet, already shivering,
and reach to grab the towel
I left hanging on the hook
outside the stall.
It's gone.

I know I'm caught
when echoes of laughter
vibrate off the cement walls.
These are not the lighthearted giggles
of a friend,
but the cackle and crow
of someone who intends
to prove his power.

I stick my head out from the plastic curtain
and Ernst stands,
smirking.

In German, he taunts me, asking,
"Need this, Hartmann?"
while twirling the towel casually in the air.
Water drips from my body,
and though I attempt to puff out my chest,
stand tall,
I can feel myself cower.

"*Gib es mir*, Ernst."
Hand it to me.

"Step out and give me a proper salute,"
he demands.
"Or has the farmer's pet
forgotten how to speak Deutsch?"
His buddies snigger behind him.

I want to rage.
Take someone down.
But I am trapped.
Naked,
alone.

I step out.
Dripping wet.
Shaking.

I salute.
Say the magic words:
"*Heil Hitler.*"

They double over in hysterics,
laugh and carry on until they're satisfied,

and then drop my towel onto the damp, dirty floor,
leave the bathhouse
as conquerors.

Still trembling,
I pick up my towel,
step back behind the curtain to dry off.
Grit on the fabric grinds
against my back, my legs.

I curse myself
for letting my guard down.
For not understanding sooner
that wearing the uniform,
risking my life,
would never guarantee me
a place inside
their party.

Claire

CHURCH, MIDWEEK

THURSDAY, SEPTEMBER 28, 1944

There once was a time
we came to church only on Sundays,
but today I put on my best dress
to attend another funeral.

I slide into the hard, wooden pew
next to Mama while Daddy, in his suit coat,
sits guarding the aisle,
as do all the fathers who are still here,
their arms draped
over the ends of the pews.

Josie will join us when she arrives by herself.
She's been working at the local diner,
but they'll put a sign out for the morning:
"Closed for funeral. Reopening at 2."
If Calvin wasn't serving overseas,
he and Josie would sit in their own pew,
but she doesn't want to sit alone.

Seats aren't assigned at church,
but they might as well be.
Just like around our dining room table,
we all take the same places every Sunday.

The empty space next to me
is where Danny should be.

Today, we're here for Mikey Sullivan.
He was twenty-three.
While Mrs. Cornelius pounds "Great Is Thy Faithfulness"
on the organ,
the Sullivan family files in silently.
First come Mikey's older sisters.
Their husbands are gone fighting
and their little ones must be in the church nursery
with a volunteer who would rather watch babies
than see the shaking shoulders of another
mother whose son will never come home.

Next are Mikey's youngest brothers, Sam and Joe.
His older brother, Rick, is somewhere
in the Pacific, holding a letter
that tells him his brother is dead.
Last down the aisle are Mikey's parents.
Mr. Sullivan grips Mrs. Sullivan's arm,
holding her up,
dragging her along.

The song ends as the family files into the first pew.
Reverend VanKampen lifts his arms,
summons us all to stand and pray.
In unison, our entire congregation rises.
The sound of more than one hundred bodies standing,
the congregation's collective weight
pierces the silence,
and then just for a moment,
before Reverend speaks,

it's so quiet
we can hear Mrs. Sullivan's ragged breaths.

On my feet, I'm relieved
to see only the backs of families that sit in front of us,
to be shielded, if only for a minute,
from the Sullivans' grief.

Karl
VERSTECKT: HIDDEN

───●──────────────────●───

THURSDAY, SEPTEMBER 28, 1944

Alone in the trees,
the silence
reminds me of the boy
I used to be. The one
who snuck off to avoid chores
in exchange for a cold swim in the stream,
the one who sat and pedaled
backward on his bike
while all the other kids laughed,
the one who spent winter nights
near the woodstove rereading
Grimm's Fairy Tales
(a book German enough
to be saved from
being banned or burned).

Some days I have to remind myself
I'm a prisoner,
serving my time.
It's easy to feel
safe in the orchard
with hundreds of apples dangling easily
within reach.

It's hard to believe
the US government supplies me
with bread and butter,
beef and potatoes, corn and peas,
while an ocean away
Mutti and my three sisters
stare at empty cupboards.

It's easy to forget
the gray skies of Germany,
the rubble in my town,
while here the sun shines
on white farmhouses
and we eat sandwiches and sip lemonade,
reclining in the shade.

It's a relief
to be assigned a guard who worries little
about his unarmed captives,
a man who hangs his gun in a tree
and naps in the sunshine
while my buddies back in Germany,
fellow soldiers
not lucky enough to be captured
slug through the mud,
guns heavy in their arms.

While I crouch under branches,
climb ladders to treetops,
twist and pull apples from branches,
my busy hands can trick my mind
into believing
that I never held a weapon,

never pulled a trigger,
never stepped over the stiff body of a dead soldier,
never had blood on my hands.

I pretend
this orchard
will hide me
forever.

Claire

LETTER FROM DANNY

———————————●

A letter from my brother arrives,
a quarter page long, his handwriting
lopsided and cockeyed across the military-issued card.
He was never good at penmanship,
but now I wonder if there's urgency, maybe anxiety
behind his scrawled words.

Doing fine,
he writes. *Not seeing much action.*
Lots of marching through mud.

He always writes on Sunday.
You're probably all eating dinner.
Maybe he's writing the words in a rush
so he won't have to think about
the meal he's missing. I imagine him
lying back on whatever is beneath him: the ground,
a rock, a cot, his knapsack.
Closing his eyes. Joining from faraway
in our family ritual
of a Sunday afternoon nap.

I know there's plenty Danny isn't saying,
plenty he can't write.
But I wish I could know

if he's collapsing exhausted into his cot
at night, or sleeping restlessly,
waking up in the darkness
homesick and more scared
than he'd ever admit out loud,
much less on paper.

I wonder if the hours move slow for him,
if he's keeping count of the days
since he left home,
if he estimates how many more
until he returns.

If he knows yet that his picking sack
now hangs on his enemy's shoulders.

If he regrets leaving,
if he realizes how good we had it
when we were little,
when we took everything
for granted,
especially each other.

Karl
KRIEG: WAR

———•————————•———

I'm bending over to lift a full crate
of Ida Reds
when I feel a smack on my back,
like a baseball that explodes,
leaving a wet ring of sticky apple juice.

I jump and turn to see Otto
three trees over, grinning.

I lean over, grab a yellowed,
bruised apple from the wet grass,
pull my arm back
and aim straight for his shoulder.

He dodges my missile at the last moment,
turns toward me,
throws his head back
and laughs before launching
another piece of fruit into the air.

Ernst, Friedrich, Walter, and Wilhelm
hear our shouts and drop their picking baskets
to join in the fight.

Rotten apples fly through the air,
and we chase each other,
ducking behind trees,
running between rows,
playing
like shadows of our younger selves,
those little boys
who once ran breathless, careless,
through the schoolyard.

Nelson, who has been lazing in the sun,
pulls himself up, leans on his elbows
to watch the fruit fight.
He shakes his head,
rubs his chin, covers a grin with his hand.

I run from tree to tree,
dodging apples,
gathering more fruit to fire,
until I take an apple hard
in the pit of my stomach.
I double over,
need a moment to catch my breath.

"Waffenstillstand! Waffenstillstand!"
I call for a truce,
cease-fire,
enough is enough!

Smiling, I wipe my sticky, wet fingers
on trousers already dripping with apple pulp
and trot back to the tall grass
where I dropped my work,

toward the apples that need
carrying to the trailer.
As I bend to pick up the wooden crate,
my smile fades.

This is how I once imagined war.

Claire

CHANCE MEETING

•————————•

SATURDAY, SEPTEMBER 30, 1944

The shouts and laughter
of the soldiers
call me out through the back door of the salesroom
where I'm helping Mama keep up.
She manages the market on weekdays,
but needs my help on Saturdays.

From a distance,
I see the men launching fruit,
ducking and covering,
freed from the chains
of a war that rages on
thousands of miles away.

I remember similar fruit fights
with Danny and Josie,
how when we were left alone in the trees,
our apple picking
always seemed to dissolve
into the same kind of mischief.

My mom's voice drags me from the memory.
"Claire, can you go find your daddy?
Let him know we're about out of McIntosh."

My feet start down the trail into the trees,
but my mind is still in the past,
remembering past fall seasons
when my older brother and sister
complained about me, the tagalong.
When I tired of their teasing
instead of being haunted by silence.

I look up to see someone coming toward me
and recognize Karl,
carrying a picking sack.

I think about turning back,
avoiding any interaction,
but tell myself to walk tall,
that I can handle myself.

"*Hallo*," he says when we are close enough
that I can see the strap on his picking sack is broken.
He's probably heading to the barn to swap it out.

"Hello. Just going to find my dad," I explain,
my eyes drawn to the wet splotches
on his shirt, his pants.

Karl notices my glance,
attempts to rub away the wet, sticky rings on his uniform.
"*Apfelkampf*," he says with a shrug.
"Throwing apples."

"I saw," I say,
and then, embarrassed to admit I was watching,

add, "My brother, sister, and I
used to do the same thing."

Rather than moving along,
Karl stays rooted, asks,
"You have a *Bruder und Schwester*?"

"My brother, Danny, is overseas,
fighting for . . ."
I hesitate. "Fighting for our side.
My sister is married and moved out;
her husband is gone to war too."

Karl's eyes show a flash of empathy,
and I can tell he's deciding
whether to say whatever's come to his mind.

He presses on:
"It must be *schwierig*—difficult—
to have us here.
As if your family has been *handelte*—
traded—for us."

I nod slowly,
then glance down the path behind him,
relieved to be saved
by the familiar cough of my dad's tractor
rounding the hill.

Karl looks over his shoulder,
and I see a flash of nervousness in his eyes.
Worry about being scolded
for fraternizing with the enemy.

The approaching tractor drowns us out
as we wave a simple goodbye,
and then head again in opposite directions.

Karl
VERURTEILT: CONVICTED

●────────────●

SUNDAY, OCTOBER 1, 1944

Sundays seems to stretch on
forever at the camp
without work to fill the hours.
Otto and I sit outside,
our backs against the wooden slats of our barracks,
reading a magazine called *TIME*.
It's dated September 11, 1944.

We stare at the glossy pictures
of smiling American troops.
Except for different uniforms,
they could be the same soldiers
we've grown up seeing in German press.

Otto asks me to read aloud.
There are stories of battles,
of enemy aircraft shot down,
of more German prisoners taken.

Each word,
each description
of that world, of the war,
feels just as close
and just as far away

as the miles
we've traveled.

My stomach is already starting to feel sick
when I come to a story
called "Murder, Inc."
My voice slows.

"Nazi Murder Camp.

Twelve-foot-high double rows
of electrically charged barbed wire;
hundreds of gaunt, man-eating dogs.

Gas chambers.

My eyes blur
and I stumble through the words.
Force myself to
keep reading.

"On one day, Nov. 3, 1943,
they annihilated
18,000 people—
Poles, Jews, political prisoners
and war prisoners."

War prisoners.
Prisoners like me.
Eighteen thousand
people
in one day.

"Human bones.
Human ashes."

When I finish the page,
we are silent
until Otto dares whisper,
"It is true."
He pauses, lowers his voice again.
"This is what we're doing
to the Jews."

I know we are both replaying the same
moment over in our minds,
the memory
we've both been pushing out of our heads
for months.

It was in France,
a dark spring morning after a battle.
We were stepping over mangled bodies
when an officer turned to us and asked,
"Do you know we are slaughtering
tens of thousands of Jews
and others unworthy of life?"

We shook our heads
in silent argument,
refusing to allow ourselves to consider
the weight of his words,
refusing to consider the roles we were playing.
Because avoiding the truth,
avoiding the responsibility

that comes with admitting the truth,
can seem a lot easier than being brave.

Since that morning,
I've continually reassured myself
that even if the worst is true,
I've no part in it.
I've only filled my requirement,
followed orders.
My path has always been set.
I've had no choices.

But this afternoon
I face reality
scratching at my soul.

The American news
sits heavy in my fingers.
The black-and-white words
linger heavy in my mouth,
spelling out a horror
I've tried to deny.

I close the magazine,
bile rising in my throat,
understanding that the truth
has chased me down,
and we deserve—
I deserve—
far worse
than a prison of trees.

Claire

UNDER THE OAK TREE

●────────●

SUNDAY, OCTOBER 1, 1944

Josie, my older sister,
should be my best friend, but sitting
under the oak she talks casually of her future,
rooted here.
Her reunion with her husband,
starting a family,
names for the babies she'll have.
Her dreams fall lightly, like the whirligigs
drifting lazily from the sky to the ground around us.

I nod, staring off into the distance
as her voice drones on.
My dreams to go to high school,
leave town,
train to be a nurse in a hospital
seem unfit to share with Josie,
would interrupt the peace of this still autumn day.

What I want feels dangerous,
like last night's storm.
The wind started quietly
when we went to bed,
but sometime in the middle of the night,
it found its strength, picked up momentum,
barreled through the darkness

with a ferociousness that uprooted
more than a dozen of Daddy's trees—
turned them over,
yanked them right out of the soil.

I am jerked back to reality
when Josie, still blabbering, asks,
"You got your eye on any cute boys
around town?"

My conversation with Karl
on the orchard path yesterday
flashes in my mind,
but I quickly push it away.

"There's no one interesting
around here," I say.

Karl

DIE RUINEN: REMAINS

●━━━━━━━━●

It's late afternoon
when Mr. D plucks me out of the orchard,
tells me to climb into the cab of his truck.
We're bouncing down the gravel trail
through the trees
when he turns down the volume on the radio
long enough
to let me know
he could use my help
in the salesroom.
"My wife and daughter
could use a bit of muscle
and an extra pair of hands."
He glances over,
returns my nod,
and then turns the music back up.

I look out the window,
and the wind blows in my face
as I watch the trees pass by.
I squeeze my shaking hands
tightly on the balls of my knees.
I'm still off-kilter.
Off-balance.
The words that Otto and I

read yesterday
still heavy on my mind,
on my heart.
The words that confirmed
that not only am I the enemy,
but an accomplice
in a plot
more vile
than I ever forced myself to consider.

I glance over at Mr. D's hands on the wheel,
and something between anger and persistence
rises out of me.
I make a decision.
If I'm being singled out
from the rest of the group,
I pledge
to prove that Germany may be my Fatherland,
but Hitler is not my father.

I pledge
to be not just the German who speaks English,
but the German who is not a Nazi.

I pledge
to be myself,
a teenager,
almost a man,
determined to do better
with the rest of his life.

We pull up next to the red, wooden barn
and Mr. D shifts the truck into park.

I suck in a heavy breath,
and make a silent promise
to them,
to myself.

I will work hard,
prove
that I may be blemished,
but I am not rotten
to the core.

Claire

QUESTIONING

Since the day I was born,
it's always been clear
that Daddy runs this orchard.
That he's the head of our house,
the boss man.
He gets his hands dirty alongside his workers,
is kind and fair,
but all things fall under his direction,
including me
and Mama.

But after school, when Daddy pops
into the salesroom to officially introduce Karl
like he's the new boy next door,
not a prisoner from Germany,
when he tells us Karl will be helping me and Mama
keep things in order,
Mama challenges him.

After he gives Karl an assignment,
I watch her follow on Daddy's heels,
chase him out to the barn
until they're standing
eye to eye.
She keeps her voice down,

but her words carry
and they sizzle.
"Do you really think
a German working in our salesroom
is good for business?
Good for your wife and daughter?"

Daddy smiles in a way
that makes me bristle,
gives Mama a tender look
that insinuates he sees her
not as his equal
but as his helper,
a convenient farmhand.
He pats her on the shoulder.
"Carolyn, trust me,
he's a nice kid, a hard worker,
and his English is good.
He might be German, but he's harmless.
Relax.
We need his help.
This is why they've sent them.
He'll be hauling apples, restocking, running errands,
not handling foreign affairs."

"Fine," Mama says,
with a deep, shaking breath.
"But if this backfires,
if something happens,
if we get complaints or lose customers,
I get to say 'I told you so.'"

"Deal," Daddy says.
He leans over, gives Mama a quick peck on the cheek,
an attempt to dispel
her frustration.

As he moves on to his next chore,
he winks over at me,
hoping to share a secret sign,
a quiet assurance
that he still has everything
under control.

I almost want to run to Mama,
join her side;
beg Daddy to listen,
prove she deserves to be heard.
But my feet freeze
and I'm stuck
wondering if maybe
Daddy could be right;
if we just need to trust,
if Karl could be nice
to have around.

Karl

ZWANGSARBEIT:
FORCED LABOR

A steady stream of customers visit
the apple market
and I do my best to earn
my right to take up space
in the salesroom,
to earn the privilege
to work beside Claire
when she resumes her role
after school each day.

But when I haul a load of apples into the salesroom,
she quickly points
from across the room
to where I should unload them.

When I am told to fill glass gallon jugs
with cold cider
fresh from the holding tank,
she is careful
to keep her distance.
Careful to wait
until I have wiped down the sides of the jug,
twisted and secured the top,

set it down, moved away,
before she'll grab it for a customer.

She'll offer a smile
to someone she's helping,
an old man or an overwhelmed mother.
Her voice is kind
when she answers a question about which variety
makes the best pie, the best sauce,
which apples travel best in a lunchbox.

But when she turns to me,
her eyes grow cloudy
and the ease in her smile fades.
The warmth of her presence
is instantly replaced
by hesitancy,
uncertainty,
an unspoken obligation
to stay on her side
of the line drawn between us.

Claire

DON'T

Don't get drawn
into his kind, blue eyes.
Don't notice the effort
he makes to speak my language,
the way he works
to twist and turn his native tongue
to build a bridge between us.

Don't encourage
his eagerness to help.
Don't look surprised
when he grabs a bushel of Ida Reds
before a customer is even done asking for them,
or restocks the cider as fast as it sells.

Don't notice
the realness of his smile,
the way the corners of his mouth
slowly turn up when he overhears a joke.
Don't pay attention
to the hopefulness in his face
when a stranger offers kind words.

Don't watch
his gaze follow the families who come to buy fruit.

Don't pay attention
to the homesickness
weighing down his shoulders as he watches
a little boy and his mother
walk together to their car.

Keep reminding yourself:
He is temporary.
Hired help.
His story is none of your business.

He's not someone
you might like
to get to know.
Not someone who might be
as lonely,
as curious,
as you.

Keep reminding yourself:
He's a German soldier,
your brother's enemy,
not fertile ground
in which to plant
a friendship.

Karl

DIE OFFENE TÜR:
THE OPEN DOOR

●━━━━━━━●

FRIDAY, OCTOBER 6, 1944

From the sinking sun in the sky
and my growling stomach,
I know it's almost quitting time.

In the distance, I hear the voices
of my comrades coming in from the orchard,
and take it as my cue
to finish up.
Claire, quiet all afternoon,
is rearranging bright red Jonathans
into baskets.
I'm about to turn the sign to Closed
when Ernst appears in the doorway.

He says roughly, *"Zeit zu gehen, Karl"*—
time to go—
and then notices Claire across the room
and whistles,
long, slow, and crude.
She pretends
she doesn't hear him,
but I see her face go red.

I'm embarrassed
for him,
for Claire,
for me.

His behavior is bad enough
at camp,
but here at the farm,
it feels uglier.

"Ernst,
raus hier."
Get out of here.

He stares me down
and growls
a German curse word
I'm glad Claire can't understand
before he turns to leave.

"I'm sorry,"
I say to Claire.

She looks nervous,
but her face softens
at my apology.
"I'm sorry
you have to live with that jerk."

I laugh and assure her
that I try to keep my distance.

"I would too," she says.

I am walking to the door
when I hear her voice once more:
"Have a good night, Karl."

My surprise
at her grace
slows my response,
and she's already turned back
to the apples
when I quietly echo,
"Gleichfalls.
You too."

Claire

DEFENSIVE

●━━━━━━━━━━●

I've done my best to avoid Karl
on the short afternoons
we've spent near each other this week,
but I knew when I walked in this morning
to prepare for a busy Saturday,
an entire day spent working alongside him,
keeping my distance would be harder.

Especially after yesterday.
Especially after his kindness
when Ernst showed up.

It's midmorning
when a young mom hurries in,
two little boys in tow.
The oldest is Tommy,
the kindergartner from school.
"Hi, Claaaaire," he bellows,
his little brother chasing him.
They both wear cowboy boots,
plaid shirts, and mischievous grins.
Tommy's mother browses the salesroom,
warning her sons
to stay close and stay still,
but they run wildly,

playing a game of tag
and touching every apple in reach.

Karl stops restocking to smile,
a soft spark of familiarity in his eyes.

Until Tommy runs right into him
and the realization
of who Karl is,
the terror of the tales told
on the school playground,
the fear of looking directly
into the face of the enemy,
grinds him to a halt.

"A German Nazi!"
Tommy screams.
Locks eyes on his little brother.
"Gary, run for your life!"

Karl returns to his work,
trying to hide his discomfort
as Tommy's mother scolds
the boys from across the room,
and I find myself
moving toward the door,
bending to trap Tommy
in a gentle hug.

"Hey, buddy.
Look at me.
It's okay. That's Karl.
He's from Germany,

but you don't have to be scared.
He's not a soldier anymore.
He won't hurt you."

Tommy wiggles his way out of my grip,
intent on playing his role
of a brave, American boy.
His finger instantly fashioned into a gun,
he points and shoots at Karl,
then ducks and runs out the door,
his brother mimicking close behind.

Tommy's mother,
red-faced and exasperated,
quickly pays for her fruit,
promising she'll get these rowdy boys out of here.
From the doorway, I watch her round up the boys
and wrangle them
into the back seat of her car.

I look down to realize
my hands are shaking.
Realize I just returned the favor.
Just defended Karl,
as he did for me.
And realize that I must turn around
and face him
in this now-empty salesroom
alone
together.

Karl

HUT SEIN: GUARD DOWN

———•———

Before another customer
can come in and ruin my chance,
I speak up.
Speak slowly,
try to get my English right.

"Claire.
Thank you.
I did not wish to scare—
what's the word?—
die Kinder."

She shrugs,
then lets a breath of laughter escape.
"I'll protect you
from the local children."

I return her smile.
"They make me remember
being a little boy
running away from Mutti,
my mother."

She pauses,
and our eyes meet

long enough that before looking away,
she finds the courage to offer a question
rather than push me away.

"If you weren't here,
if there was no war,
where would you be, Karl?"

I am distracted
by the softness in her voice
as she calls me by name,
but I press myself to answer
a question I haven't had the chance
to consider.

"I'd like to think I'd be in school,"
I confess,
"but all my plans changed
once I was put in charge
of providing food for *die Familie* table.
So I would probably
be working in the store of my
mother's brother.
My *Onkel*."

She nods and tilts her head slightly,
then notices a car pulling in
and decides our conversation
must finish.

"Maybe you'll find a way,
after the war."
Then quickly adds,

"I'm going to high school,
and then I'm going to be a nurse."

I want to say more,
to tell her I believe she'll do it,
but she's already moved on
to help the customer.
Breaking the spell
cast by two teenagers
from enemy countries
speaking a common language.

Claire

AFTER-SCHOOL SNACK

——●————————●——

As soon as I'm home from school,
I change into my work clothes,
head out to the salesroom.
My mom finishes ringing up a sale
and then asks me to take over
so she can finish the laundry,
start dinner.

My stomach is growling,
so before I get to work
I grab a Baldwin from a basket,
rub the apple against
my pant leg until its thick skin shines,
and take a bite.

My mouth is full
when Karl comes through the door,
pulling a wagon of Red Delicious.
I cover my full mouth
and he laughs.
"*Essen die* profits?" he asks.

Instead of defending myself,
I finish chewing, smile back,
and motion to the baskets

around him.
"Go ahead,
have one too."

I expect him to decline,
to wave my offer away,
to stay focused on his work,
but he leans over,
grabs a fresh-picked apple,
and raises it in the air
like he's giving a toast,
before joining me
for an afternoon snack.

Karl

NACHRICHTEN: NEWS

———•———•———

Claire and I are chomping on our apples
when I remember the newspaper clipping
in my pocket.

I set down my half-eaten fruit
on a bench,
wipe my sticky hands on my pants
before reaching to retrieve it.

I unfold the thin paper,
offering it to her.

"Found this yesterday
while reading the newspapers
back at the camp.
Thought of you."

She looks surprised
but curious,
and reaches to take the paper
from my hands.

It's a story I tore from the local paper.
An account of a nurse
on the battlefield,

one I thought
she'd find interesting.

Her eyes scan the article,
and as they do
I reconsider its contents,
the story about a young woman
forced to do a job bigger
than anything she was trained for,
a story about the bleeding men brought in
from the battlefield.

When I read it yesterday,
I only thought about Claire's dream
to be nurse,
her ambition.
I only thought of finding a way
to connect,
show her I'm listening.

A flash of worry comes over me.
I didn't think
of her brother.
I didn't consider Danny,
that when she reads
about wounded American soldiers,
she must see only his face.

Her eyes are focused
on the paper but I can see
them cloud.
I break her long silence.
"You can *lessen*—read—it later."

Claire pauses,
finishes the line she's on,
but then nods,
slowly folds the article back up,
and sticks it in her own pocket.

I expect her to say something
about the war or school,
about her brother, her own family,
but again she turns the attention
back to me.

"Your family, Karl,
back home—
they know you're safe here?"

I exhale heavily.
Think of the letters I've sent
Mutti, my sisters.

"*Ja*, they do," I say.

She nods,
tosses her finished apple
into the trash.
"That must be nice."

I nod.
A good response doesn't exist.
There aren't words
to sweeten
the sour reality
of this war.

I'm still trying to think
of something worth saying
when Mr. D strides in.

"How's it going?" he asks,
scanning the room,
making sure things are in order.

Claire lies for both of us,
for all of us.
"Everything's good, Dad."

I glance down at my half-eaten apple,
quickly pick it up,
and toss it in the trash beside Claire's core,
feeling guilty
about letting something so good
go to waste.

Claire

INTERRUPTION

TUESDAY, OCTOBER 10, 1944

I'm bent over an algebra problem when we hear a
quick knock on the schoolhouse door.

Pete barges in, locates me with his eyes.
"Excuse me, miss, I need
to take Claire home."
He stands at the door,
fidgeting with the dirty cap he's taken off his head,
his eyes flitting nervously.

Pete coming to pick me up cannot mean anything good.

Miss VerWys stands,
smooths her voice like she smooths her dress.
"Yes, of course, Pete."

My heart pounds and my fingers go numb.
I scoop up my books and scattered papers,
toss them into my bag and throw it over my shoulder,
though Miss VerWys tells me I can leave
my things, get them later.
Other students whisper and wonder.

I know somehow that this knock will be a marker in
my life:

that years later, everything leading up to this day
will be the *before*,
and whatever waits for me at home
will be the *after*.

Karl

AMERIKANISCHE FLUGZEUGE: AMERICAN PLANES

●━━━━━━━━●

TUESDAY, OCTOBER 10, 1944

I've been left alone
to work in the barn
this morning;
everyone else seemingly disappeared.

The silence
gives me too much time
to think, to remember.

I sort apples
like I sort through memories,
my mind returning
to a morning in France.
A world away
but only a few months ago.

On the battlefield, we hid
as American planes flew overhead.
Though it wasn't bombs that dropped,
but leaflets.
Paper flitting down in the wind,
bearing General Eisenhower's scrawled signature
and a promise:

"The German soldier who carries this safe conduct pass
is using it as a sign of his genuine wish
to give himself up.
He is to be disarmed,
to be well-looked after;
to receive food and medical attention
as required,
and to be removed
from the danger zone
as soon as possible."

We read.
Debated.

"It's a trick," some repeated.
"A hoax.
Trust the enemy,
end up dead."

"Maybe it's a ticket out,"
others dared to whisper,
maybe more optimistic,
more tired,
or more homesick.

I looked up,
wondering how bombs and promises
could fall from the same sky.

Claire

PANIC

———————

TUESDAY, OCTOBER 10, 1944

"What's wrong?"
I ask Pete
once the schoolhouse door is closed
and we've turned
quickly down the path to the house.

The grass is still wet from
the early morning dew,
and my socks and shoes
grow more damp with each step.

"I'm going to let your mama and daddy
talk to you, Claire."
He won't look me in the eyes
as he jogs beside me.

I hand him my book bag
and run.

Karl

WEISSE FLAGGE: WHITE FLAG

Still sorting,
deciding what apples are nice enough
to be put on display
and which ones are best for cider,
my mind now wanders
to the day the Americans encircled us.

We were marching,
just miles from glimpsing the French coast,
when we were forced to raise our white flags.
Looking back now,
I can admit
my first instinct
was relief.

I no longer cared about winning;
I wanted it to be over.
I wanted to go home.

An American soldier attempted to speak
my language: *"Hände hoch, Hände hoch!"*
Hands up.
He screamed and pantomimed orders.

I dropped my gun to the ground,
glad to be rid of its weight,
raised my empty hands into the air.
Watched as my fellow soldiers did the same.

The American must not have known the German words
for "on your knees,"
so instead communicated this
with the butt of his gun,
moving down the line
with quick blows to our shoulders
that sent our knees crashing
into the gravel.

In my mind, I heard the officers who trained me
screaming, *"Drückeberger"*—
coward,
slacker,
quitter.

Now close enough
to feel the hot breath of the enemy's anger
sprayed in our faces,
we were searched and disarmed.
The eyes of the boy who came to search me
met mine
for half a moment,
long enough to recognize
a flash of fear
masked behind the fury of his performance.
Like the pause of a boy on his first hunting trip,
his long-awaited prey finally within range,
now uncertain

if he really wants to shoot
the animal standing,
breathing,
in front of him.

Ordered to stand,
to march,
we turned back to the road we had come from,
our eyes no longer focused high on the horizon
but down on our boots.
The Americans swaggered beside us
holding their guns,
weapons that made them grow taller,
that gave them the power to laugh at us,
prisoners in their possession.

I'm uncertain if my heart
beat louder from keeping my hands
stretched above my head
or from fear
that flanked us.

I avoided thinking
about what might come next.
Instead, I dreamed
about the luxury of sleeping
in a bed.
I imagined a bath,
scrubbing my hair,
rinsing the dust off my face,
pulling on dry socks.
I allowed my thoughts to drift to mornings
when Mutti called me in

from the barn for breakfast.
How she came behind me
at the table and set a warm biscuit
with strawberry jam in front of me.
How she stopped
to squeeze my shoulder
before turning back
wordlessly to the stove.

I walked and forced myself to believe
that just being alive
was enough
for now.

Claire

WHAT NO ONE NEEDS
TO SAY ALOUD

•————————•

TUESDAY, OCTOBER 10, 1944

I slow when I get to the front porch.
Through the screen door, I see
everyone gathered, heads down in the living room:
Josie,
Mama,
Daddy.

The sight of Daddy on the couch
instead of working in the orchard
on a Tuesday morning
is a sure confirmation
our world has stopped spinning.

The door squeaks and everyone looks up,
except Mama,
whose face is in her hands.

Their eyes are red.
I collapse into Daddy's arms
and know.

Karl

BLUT UND EHRE:
BLOOD AND HONOR

● ━━━━━━━━━━━━ ●

TUESDAY, OCTOBER 10, 1944

Still no sight of Pete, Mr. D, or Nelson.
I pour another bushel of apples
onto the sorter
and my memory marches on,
as we did on that afternoon of our capture.

After slogging for more than an hour,
my throat felt like a desert,
my shoulders throbbed.
My arms,
still raised in surrender,
sagged like a tired scarecrow.

The guards told us to halt.
We were in a clearing now,
a makeshift military outpost
on what looked to be the remains of an old farm.
In front of the stone wall of a barn
the Americans patted us down again,
taking whatever they could find.

One collected watches.
Laughing loudly,

he threw his fist into the air,
seven or eight heirlooms bound
tightly around his arm.

I watched as the silver
flashed in the sun,
and knew that any treasure
they could strip off of us
would be worth more to them
than our bodies—than our souls.

Because I know English,
I was the one who understood their screams,
their accusations,
their demands
for revenge.

An officer yelled and weaved through us,
stopping randomly
to point a finger into
the ten chests of those who would pay.
I stared straight ahead.
Willed myself to disappear.
Next to me, I could feel Otto
shaking. His boots tapped
the dusty ground in a nervous rhythm
that made my heart beat faster.

When an officer came close to me,
I felt his breath in my face,
his finger on my chest.
I felt him pull me forward by the shirt

to stand next to nine others.
Some shouting,
some crying,
some stoic.

I heard a command,
I heard ammunition load.
I thought I heard a hot bullet searing toward my head.

I prayed to a God I rarely believe in
until I need him.
I prayed Mutti would be able to take the news.
I prayed that when they shot, I'd be first,
so I wouldn't have to feel the others
fall beside me.

I never asked my comrades
how long we stood there,
whether it was two hours or two minutes.
How long they watched us wait to die.

I didn't hear the barking voice
that gave me back my life.
I just felt my friends grab and lift me
around the armpits,
my muscle memory
still stunned
from the machine gun pointed
at my head moments before.

Blut und Ehre.
Blood and honor.

The Hitler Youth embossed these words
on my belt buckle,
engraved them on my pocketknife.

But this afternoon,
there was no *Blut und Ehre*,
blood or honor,
only humiliation
and fear.

Claire

WESTERN UNION

Washington, DC

Tuesday, October 10, 1944

Mr. Saul DeBoer
2505 8th Avenue, Apeldoorn, MI

The Secretary of War desires me to express his heartfelt
regret that your son, Corporal Daniel DeBoer, was
killed in action on the eighteenth of September in
France. Confirming letter follows.

Ulio, the Adjutant General

Karl

VERSCHLIMMBESSERUNG:
[NO TRANSLATION TO ENGLISH]

Closest definition: an attempt to help
that only makes things worse

It's nearly lunchtime
and I'm carrying a crate of Seconds to the cooler
when Nelson walks into the barn.
His face is weathered,
his mouth serious,
his eyes worried.

"Karl, finish up in here
and head on over to the truck.
We're loading up;
calling it an early day."

I look out at the bright sky,
confused.
I don't see a storm coming.
"Warum denn so?"
I question. "Why?"

"The family here has had a . . ."
He pauses too long.

"Tragedy.
We need to give them space."

I stack the rest of the waiting crates
and then step out of the barn.
The deafening silence
of the usually humming orchard
puts a pit in my stomach.

As I head up the hill to find the truck,
I scan the farmhouse,
looking for clues
of what has gone wrong,
when I catch a glimpse
of Claire's blond hair.
She sits on an old tree swing
in the backyard, her face turned away
toward the trees.

I look around to make sure
no one is watching me
and then approach slowly.
Not wanting to scare her,
I softly call her name
from an arm's length away:
"Claire?"

She glances back for an instant,
just long enough for me to see
her red, puffy eyes,
then shakes her head
and waves me away.

I pause, then try again:
"Claire, are you okay?"

"No," she says,
her voice short, hoarse, tired.
"I'm not.
A telegram came today.
Danny is dead."

My stomach drops and
I search for words,
then I hear the truck start up
and know Nelson is hurrying me.

"Claire, I'm so . . ."
but I can't find the right words,
especially ones in a different language.

"Please, Karl, just go,"
Claire says, her voice drained of emotion—
still staring into the horizon,
still not looking at me.
I turn to leave,
aware I don't belong here,
not now,
maybe not ever.

I feel like I'm going to be sick
as I climb into the back of the truck.
Everyone is waiting, silent.
I avoid looking at faces
and take my seat next to Otto.

As we slowly pull out of the driveway,
I avoid glancing at the farmhouse as we pass,
knowing it holds Claire's parents,
raw with grief.
Claire's anguished words
still ring in my head.

As we pick up speed,
I try to remind myself:
I wasn't the one
who pulled the trigger
or drove the tank
or dropped the bomb
that killed Danny.

It's not my fault
I was born German.
I have only followed orders,
done what I've been told.

I have always been given plenty of good reasons
to sign up,
stand up,
stand tall,
fight,
belong,
believe.

But as my mind flashes to Claire's face
I realize:
like dead, dry branches on a tree,
none of those reasons
hold weight anymore.

151

Claire

ENDINGS

●————————————●

WEDNESDAY, OCTOBER 11, 1944

Of course
he died
with the first
whispers of autumn,
when all things
at their pinnacle of beauty
succumb to ruin.

When leaves turn
fiery orange and crimson red
and then let go of their branches.

When an apple ripens and rounds
to its fullest
and then is torn
from its limb,
or worse,
rustled by a careless picker,
tumbles,
hidden in the tall grass
where it will rot
alone.

Karl

GESCHLOSSEN: SHUTTERED

——————•——————

WEDNESDAY, OCTOBER 11, 1944

I didn't sleep much last night,
but this morning
Pete is back here at the camp
right on time.
The farm truck ready
to take us to the work
the DeBoers won't
be able to face today.

The air bites this morning,
so Otto and I don't mind
the close quarters
as we bump and thump
down the gravel road,
hugging our arms,
wishing for warmer jackets,
sitting close enough against each other
to share body heat.
A few close their eyes, drop their heads,
doze off to the rhythm of the road.

We've come to know this trip by its landmarks:
the big oak on the corner,
the general store,

train tracks,
wooden houses that might blow over with a stiff wind.

The apple-shaped sign waves us into the orchard drive.
The blinds of the farmhouse
are closed.

The sky is gray and the breeze bites us
as we climb out of the truck.
No one speaks.

Walter sees it first,
bumps my chest with his arm and points:
the gold star in the window.
From newspaper articles, we've learned
it's a sign
this family deserves
extra respect
and sympathy.

The Closed sign still hangs on the salesroom,
and Pete tells me I'll join the others
out in the trees.
I won't need to be
up here by the barns,
next to the house,
near Claire.

Relief washes over me,
just as it did the first day
I arrived on this orchard
and realized I'd been given

an easier assignment,
a way out.

Guilt replaces the place
in my heart
where integrity
should be.

Claire

CASEROLES AND CONDOLENCES

●━━━━━━━━━━━●

WEDNESDAY, OCTOBER 11, 1944

Danny's funeral is the day after tomorrow.
Three church ladies stop by
to hug Mama, pat my shoulder,
drop off casseroles and condolences,
stammer to find the right words, assurances
about God's plan
and perfect providence,
about everything happening for a reason.
Though they all remember,
they don't mention Mama's first baby boy,
who they watched her bury.
They don't acknowledge
that Mama has no sons left.
That she will soon have as many gravestones
as she does children still living.

Mrs. Sullivan stops too,
but instead of words,
she and Mama just share tears
and the bitter truth
that they now belong to the same club
of mothers who have lost sons
to the war.

Since I came running
home from school yesterday,
Mama hasn't said one word
to me. We move heavily
near each other,
she leans around me
to place a dish into the sink,
shuffles past my room
on her way to the bathroom,
looks down
when Daddy escapes to the barn—
his work an excuse
to get some fresh air
and leave me alone
to bear the stench
of her agony.

They leave me alone
to carry the weight
that I, a girl, someone
they don't expect to carry on
the family name
or take over the family farm,
am alive,
while their sons
are dead.

Karl
HERBEIGERUFEN: SUMMONED

THURSDAY, OCTOBER 12, 1944

The evening before Danny's funeral,
we're back at camp,
dusty, dirty, tired,
piling out of the back of the truck,
when Nelson whistles.
"Gather round, boys."
We glance at each other and huddle
in a semicircle around him.

"Been thinking.
Seems only right that I pay my respects,
go to the boy's funeral tomorrow.
Maybe it would be fitting for
you all to be there.
Be good for you to be in a church again,
see another side of the nastiness
of this war.
God knows none of you are blameless."

He takes a heaving breath
and pauses
long enough to make me notice
my jumble of thoughts
traveling down

to the pit
of my stomach.

"I know you don't have fancy clothes to wear—
just clean up best you can.
I'm not aiming to make a scene,
but I can't right leave you
alone on the farm."

I think of the DeBoers,
of Claire sitting alone on that swing,
of her asking me to go away.

I've been taught to accept orders
without question,
but every way I turn it around in my mind,
the thought of German soldiers
paying their respects at an American boy's funeral
seems like a poor idea.
Nelson may have an appreciation for peacemaking,
but a funeral doesn't seem like the time
or the place.

There's no room for discussion.
We are dismissed to the barracks
to wash for dinner.
I'm trudging toward the bunkhouse
when Otto turns to catch my eye,
trying to decide
if there's anything worth saying.
Ernst, three steps ahead of us, jeers
loud enough for all to hear,

"Lucky us.
All it took was one more dead American
and we get out of work in the morning."
Anton and Heinz laugh, jab each other's sides.

I am silent.
I don't speak up
or defend the DeBoers.
Or rush at Ernst and pound him into the ground.

Instead, my face goes red
as the good sense in my head
begs me to say something,
and my conscience nags at me,
asking what it will take for me
to risk getting noticed,
risk getting in trouble,
risk finding the guts
to do what's right.

Claire

PLAYING

THURSDAY, OCTOBER 12, 1944

The night before Danny's funeral,
I lie in bed
remembering
when we were younger
and my cousins came over to play.
We ran out to the trees, found a clearing to set up camp,
pretended that our parents were missing
and we were surviving on our own.

After gathering fallen-down tree branches
to build forts, I wandered off
with the girls to pick dandelions
and Queen Anne's lace, arrange the wildflowers
alongside pods of milkweed
stripped to look like fish fillets,
while Danny and the other boys
whittled sticks, fashioned guns
to play war.
They ran around, chasing each other,
aiming and making popping noises,
pretending to grab their chests
and fall dead.

The other girls and I sighed and fussed,
annoyed, begging them to drop their weapons

and come home for dinner,
preaching that war was not the game
we wanted to play.
I remember Danny ruffling my hair,
telling me to loosen up,
stop worrying so much,
assuring me that someday he'd grow up
and I'd finally be rid of him.

What cruelty
to look back now and know
that those pretend battles,
dramatic deaths,
and teasing advice
were actually rehearsal
for my future.

Karl
BEGRÄBNIS: FUNERAL

It's midmorning when the truck pulls to a stop
in the crowded church parking lot.
I'm glad we are late enough
that no one watches us
lumber out of its bed,
windblown and underdressed.

The church is orange brick;
a handful of stairs lead up to its entrance.
Compared to the ancient, towering cathedrals
of Germany,
it's tiny,
like a toy miniature.
Everything in this country
looks like it was built yesterday.

I keep my eyes on my boots.
I'm wearing a white button-down shirt
over my work shirt.
At least my pants are clean.

A sudden pang of homesickness
pierces my stomach
as my feet climb the church steps.
It's been more than a year

since I last walked into my church
with my mother, my sisters.
Emmie, the youngest, gripping my hand.

We file in, shoulders back,
posing
as fearless soldiers.
I attempt
to steady
my shaking legs.

Claire

FUNERAL, FRONT ROW

●————————————————●

The organ plays a slow, sad march
as we enter the sanctuary
single file.
I walk behind Daddy,
keeping my eyes squared on his back,
his black suit coat moving steadily ahead.
I avoid the somber glances
of my friends and neighbors.
I don't have to see their faces
to know their eyes
drip sympathy.

We pass the wooden pew
in the sanctuary's center that
my family has taken up all my life,
instead parade forward to one in the very front.
I'm aware of Danny's absence,
the space he should be taking up
beside me,
the people watching who will no longer
think of our family
as who we are,
but who we are missing.

Karl
BALKON: BALCONY

●────────●

FRIDAY, OCTOBER 13, 1944

I immediately recognize
the song the organ plays
as we are swept
through the church's wide-swinging doors.
The irony of hearing a hymn
composed hundreds of years ago in Germany
would almost make me laugh
if I wasn't so uncomfortable.

It strikes me how enemies
sing the same songs to the same God.
How one side's prayers for deliverance
equal loss and destruction
for the other.

Nelson points us to stairs leading to a balcony.
He said we'd be in the back row,
but the wooden doors of the sanctuary
are already closed.
I'm grateful the music
covers the sound of our entry. We slide down
into a single row, overlooking the congregation.
A few people glance up behind them, see us;
some stop to gawk,
others quickly flick their eyes back to the altar.

One little boy turns clear around,
stares freely
until his mom pinches his shoulder.
She keeps her hand on his back,
a warning.

The DeBoers are in the front row.
They wear black.
Suits and dresses.
Claire and her mother sing with their heads down.
Mr. D holds a songbook out in front of them.
His dusty brown hair is slicked back,
covers a bald spot I can see from above.
I'm not sure I'd recognize him
in a suit instead of farm clothes,
without a dingy cap shielding his face.

When I look at Claire,
I see her strong back,
but can almost feel the weight
on her shoulders.
As if her pain transfers to me,
I remember Vati's funeral.
Eyes boring into my back.
I was only twelve,
and people kept assuring me
it would be okay to cry,
but how do you cry
when you're already underwater?

Claire

FUNERAL, FRONT ROW, II

●━━━━━━━━●

FRIDAY, OCTOBER 13, 1944

Reverend VanKampen, as if he can will God's presence
to come down,
raises his arms in invocation and recites Psalm 46.
The loud certainty of his voice startles me.

"God is our refuge and strength,
a very present help in trouble.
Therefore, we will not fear,
though the earth be removed,
and though the mountains be carried
into the midst of the sea;
though the waters thereof roar and be troubled,
though the mountains shake with the swelling thereof."

I wonder about Danny,
how he felt the first time he saw the Atlantic.
I wonder if he ever saw mountains,
if he stretched his eyes to find any beauty
in that war.
If he stretched his eyes to find any beauty
on the other side of that ocean.

My head is too full, my thoughts too distracted
to allow me to digest the sermon.
I've heard these words spoken before

at the funerals of other boys
and men who won't be coming home.
Words about baptism and promise,
heaven, the arms of Jesus, and
hope.

There is no body.

No coffin.

I wonder who dug Danny's grave.
I wonder if they buried him with his boots on.
I wonder if the person who laid his body
down said a prayer
or just cussed
as he placed another boy in a hole.

Karl

BALKON: BALCONY, II

———●———

FRIDAY, OCTOBER 13, 1944

The preacher pretends not to see us.
His eyes, under wide-rimmed glasses,
stay steady on his people.
He reads Scripture
and then talks long. He holds the Bible
like it's a weapon in his right hand,
shaking it up and down while he speaks
but never opening it.

The way words fall easily off his tongue,
I can tell he's said them before.

We sit above
these people,
not within them,
up where it's easier
to observe,
stay distant,
rationalize.
To remind ourselves:
This is war.
There are dead sons
on both sides.

In the first days my feet walked
American ground,
it seemed war had left this place
untouched. That these lucky Americans
got to wave their flags
and promote their propaganda
thousands of miles from the fighting,
thousands of miles from the dead bodies.
Never having to look out their windows
to see a tank roll by,
or waking up to the rhythm of boots
marching down their streets.

But now my eyes are drawn
to the dull ache
etched on Claire's face.
I wish I could have kept the war
from her, kept her
protected
from the pain.
I wish the brother
she's grown used to missing
wouldn't forever be as far away
as the battles,
bombings,
and blood
I now hope
she'll never have to witness.

Claire

FUNERAL, FRONT ROW, III

———•————————•———

FRIDAY, OCTOBER 13, 1944

Reverend says Amen
and we stand in unison to sing.
From the balcony there is a sudden smack,
the heavy fall of a hymnbook
like a clap of thunder,
like an explosion.

We all turn around to see the
~~Germans,~~
~~POWs~~
Nazis from the farm
peering over us.
Ernst, who likely dropped the hymnbook,
is bending to retrieve it.
He and his friends not even able to hide
the smirks on their faces.

We've been taught only to whisper in church,
but Mama, next to me,
has no restraint left.
She shouts,
"What are they doing here?
Get them out.
Out!"

Her trembling voice echoes heavily
over the rows of the shocked congregation.

Reverend's face turns ghostly white,
and the organist fumbles with her song sheet.
Reverend looks to his left
and, flustered, directs her to keep playing.
The first measures of the hymn
cover the murmuring,
the shaking heads,
the curses.

I know I should turn completely forward,
face the altar, the cross,
and sing,
but I keep my shoulders twisted,
ensure my scowl is noticed
by every pair of shifting German eyes.

When I get to Karl,
his eyes already on me,
I pause,
glare longer,
make sure he knows
that his kind eyes
and sympathy
won't fix this.
Make sure he understands
this is his cue
to leave.

Karl
BALKON: BALCONY, III

●————————————————————●

I want to disappear
when the hymnbook drops,
when every eye turns upon us
and I'm reminded of who we are,
why we have no right
to be here.

It's Ernst,
of course,
who dropped it.
Who thought it'd be funny.
Anton and Heinz who laugh along
because they are trained monkeys
who play the part of loyal sidekicks.

My anger flashes,
not at Ernst, Anton, or Heinz,
but at Nelson.
What did he expect,
bringing us here?
How did he think this would go?
We are German soldiers
at the funeral of a boy killed
by our fire.

Nelson jerks his arm
in anger, motioning us out,
warning us
not to cause any more drama.

As we scramble from the pew,
I turn to find Claire's eyes
in the front row,
attempt to send a silent apology
from afar,
but when her eyes find mine,
they only hold contempt.

The muffled sounds
of another hymn accompany us
as we shuffle down
the balcony's back stairs.
Voices sing
and echo
that all is well.

We pile into the back of the truck,
Nelson cursing and muttering
as he climbs into the driver's seat,
rehearsing the lecture we'll get
back at the farm.

We're bouncing down the gravel road
before the benediction,
before the family can make their slow procession
up the aisle.
My face is red,

my embarrassment
now turning to anger.
Because once again
who I am
will be determined by the group I belong to.
And my comrades
can't pretend,
even for a few minutes,
to be decent.

Or maybe I'm a fool
for believing
that I had any hope
of persuading Claire,
of persuading myself,
that I am different.

Claire

FUNERAL, FRONT ROW, IV

●━━━━━━━━●

Daddy holds the hymnal out in front of me.
His hand is shaking, but he tries to steady it.
His low voice blends with the voices of the congregation.

When peace, like a river, attendeth my way,
When sorrows like sea billows roll;
Whatever my lot, thou hast taught me to say,
"It is well,
it is well with my soul."

I move my lips,
but sound does not come out.

Something inside
won't let me sing a lie.

Karl
KRÄHEND: CROWING

Everyone played silent and sorrowful
while Nelson chewed us out,
assured us we played the part
of the enemy to a T,
confirmed everyone's suspicions
about the good-for-nothing, evil Germans.

Back at camp in the mess hall,
the commotion we caused
becomes a joke,
a reason to brag and banter,
a badge of honor.
At the crowded dinner table,
Anton, Ernst, and Heinz
rehash the story of the dropped hymnal
to POWs sitting nearby
who work at other farms.

"You should have seen the family's faces."
Ernst doesn't wait to finish his mouthful of potatoes
as he talks, throws his head back,
and cackles as he recounts the scene.

"Everyone in the whole church
turned around," Anton chimes in.

"The preacher got all tongue-tied
and the organist froze."
He pantomimes the organist, his fingers banging
out an imaginary tune and then suspending
in midair. He stops laughing long enough
to mimic her dropped jaw
and wide eyes.

I glance at Otto sitting beside me.
He leans away
from the table,
drops his fork,
swallows hard.
If anyone believes
this performance doesn't deserve laughter,
they lack the courage to speak up.

Including me.

Claire

INVADERS

●━━━━━━━●

The busiest days on an orchard
are sunny Saturdays in October.
Everyone wants to bite into a fresh-off-the-tree apple
on a day like today,
when the blue sky sings
with hope. I'm expected
to pop out of bed at dawn,
be in the salesroom by eight a.m.
to greet customers
who wonder what kinds of apples keep the longest,
feel the necessity for small talk
about sugar rationing and sour pies,
and want help toting cider to their cars.

Yesterday, we mourned
my brother.
Today, I'm asked to serve,
to smile.
To get up while my mother stays in bed,
because it's assumed her grief
at losing her second son
must be greater than mine.

The customers who read about my dead brother
in the newspaper obituary

or sat with us
yesterday in church
tread lightly, curious
to see how we're holding up.
They study my eyes when they think I'm not looking,
paint "I'm-so-sorry" expressions on their faces,
pat my back while sighing deeply,
ask how my mother is doing,
and hope their sympathy
has the power to fix
what's broken.

The Open sign invites people
to flock here today,
to intrude on our family,
to trespass freely,
gawk at our house,
flood our farm.
If I could, I'd snap that sign around,
declare us Closed.
Make them all go away.

Instead, like apples boiled down to sauce,
I simmer.
A slow resentment raging
against an Earth
that doesn't have the decency
to slow its turning
even for one day.

Karl

AUSVERKAUFT: OUT OF STOCK

●————————————●

After picking all morning,
we sit under the trees to eat
salami and tough bread
carried with us from camp.
No one expects any special lunches
to be served today.

Mr. D drives up on his tractor,
tells us to finish up
and then load the apples we've picked.
We lug and stack heavy wooden crates
filled to the brim onto his trailer.

"We're busy today
and the market is emptying out quickly,"
he says, pointing to Otto and Wilhelm.
"You two hop on the trailer and join me in the barn;
I need your help sorting."
Then he motions to me.
"Karl, I need you back in the salesroom.
My wife isn't ready to face people
and Claire can't keep up alone."

The mention of Claire's name
ties my stomach in knots.

When Mr. D turns to jump onto the tractor,
Ernst slaps me on the back.
"Viel Spaß mit der Apfelprinzessin,"
he whispers. *Enjoy the Apple princess.*

Rage springs up in me
and my fist instinctively
clenches into a tight ball.
But I turn away,
do as I'm told,
and leap onto the back of the trailer.

We bounce through the trees,
the wind and tractor exhaust in our faces
until we pull into the drive
and up to the squat wooden building
where the apples are sold.
Mr. D stalls the tractor long
enough for me to jump off.

Cars are parked next to the market
on the gravel driveway
shared with the DeBoer house,
and customers trickle out of the salesroom
with arms filled with fruit.
Pete zips from the barn on a forklift,
dropping off a skid of apples,
looking at me and jerking his head
toward the salesroom to let me know
they are ready for display.

I hoist a half bushel of Empires and
lug them into the salesroom,

in search of their place
on a tiered,
wooden bench
labeled with their name and price.
Claire is standing at the money box,
waiting on an old woman bent over her pocketbook,
counting change to drop into her hand.

Even from across the room,
the air hangs thick and awkward
between us.
I don't need to get any closer
to know she will
protect her space,
leave little room for me
to offer another apology
for my fellow soldiers,
for what Ernst did yesterday,
for the nameless German who killed her brother.

I set the heavy apples down,
the sound of that falling hymnbook
still echoing in my ears,
replaying the image of Claire's face
as she turned around in the front pew
to look up, her face
lined with pain.

I start outside to grab more apples,
and she waits
until I've gone
before greeting another customer at the door.

I curse under my breath,
understanding that gap between us
has been wrenched farther open.
Whatever trust I'd earned,
whatever grace I'd been given,
whatever forgiveness I'd been granted
is gone.

Claire

TOO SOON

When I open my eyes this morning,
there is a split second
when I forget,
when my heart isn't crushed
by remembering
that Danny is dead.

But then reality crashes
over me. My brother won't ever come home.
Even when the war is over,
he won't burst through the door.
Pick me off the floor,
twirl me around in a giant hug.

Rather than allow myself
to lie still and feel any more pain,
I push my heartache aside,
and like a good farmer's daughter,
get up to work.
Mama's grief takes precedence
over my own,
and Daddy's got plenty to do,
which leaves me
to sell the apples,

work the salesroom,
do my part.

And avoid Karl.

It's harder today.
It's quieter on a Monday morning,
fewer customers to fill the space
between us.

He is first to shatter the silence.
"No school for you today?"

I can still hear Daddy's words Sunday night
as I laid out my dress.
"I know I promised before, Claire-bug,
but things are different now."

I shrug.
"I'm needed here."

He sets down his work,
turns to look directly at me,
begging me to meet his eyes:
"I'm sorry, Claire."

His words
hang heavy
in the chilly morning air.

I don't want to hear
the pain in his voice,

I don't want to recognize
the aching in his eyes.
I know I could accept
his sympathy,
acknowledge it's not his fault:
the scene in the church,
that Danny's dead
and he's not.

But it's too soon.
Fresh grief and bitterness
cloud my heart,
spring up on my tongue,
and I turn in the opposite direction.

"Sorry doesn't fix anything, Karl."

Karl

ZU SPÄT: TOO LATE

●————————————————●

MONDAY, OCTOBER 16, 1944

For the rest of the day,
I keep my mouth shut
and do my job.

How could I have thought
that Claire would be ready
for an apology?

If there was ever a chance
to get out,
to resist,
to protest,
to turn away
from the mess this war has got me into—
if there was ever a chance
to become the kind of man
I'd always thought I would be—
it was a million missteps
and wrong turns
ago.

Claire

PUNISHED

——————●——————

It's still dark
when I am woken
by the sounds of Daddy getting ready
to head out to work.

I know I need to get up too.
Do the same.
Put on my warm work clothes
instead of my school dress.

For years, I've heard Mama say
that she is living Daddy's dream.
That the day he took the job of running this orchard,
when they were young and first married,
he decided her fate as well.

But giving up my dreams,
having to quit school
like every other woman in my family has done,
feels more a life sentence
than a sacrifice.

Mama isn't the only one
who lost Danny.

As I throw my legs over my bed
and my bare feet hit the cold farmhouse floor,
I curse how unfair it is
that I'm being punished
for being too strong.

Karl

SPIEL UND SPASS:
FUN AND GAMES

———●———————●———

TUESDAY, OCTOBER 17, 1944

In the dusk after dinner,
we head to the field
to squeeze in a quick game
of soccer.
I'm facing off,
smashing shins with Ernst,
when I knock him to the ground.

The ball kicked downfield,
I bend to help him up.
But he shakes his head.
Refuses my outstretched hand.
"Weichei"—
sissy—he spits.
"Don't act like you're one of us.
We know you're more interested
in making friends with that farm girl
than fighting for *der Führer.*
When Germany wins,
the truth will come out."

Back on his feet, he shoves my chest,
runs toward the ball.

Leaves me breathless
and alone
on the sideline.

Claire

DETACHED

●━━━●

Karl seems to have given up
on trying to convince me
he's worth talking to,
just as I've given up
on my dream of ever going back to school.

It's lonely out here in the salesroom—
just me and the apples,
separated from their trees,
waiting to be purchased and hauled away.
I wouldn't mind someone to talk to,
but every time I see Karl's face,
I think of Danny.

The thought has crossed my mind,
how well the two of them would have gotten along.
I dare to consider
how the three of us
might have laughed and chatted,
become friends
if Karl's army hadn't killed Danny first.

And so Karl and I ignore any spark
of friendship,
any hope of peace.

We maneuver around each other,
work to avoid each other's eyes,
try to accept what is,
even though nothing
is as it should be.

Because just like everything else in my life,
I have no power
to fix it.

Karl

DIE NACHZÜGLER:
THE STRAGGLERS

●━━━━━●

The salesroom is slow and fully stocked
when Mr. D stops in,
tells Claire, "I'm going to steal Karl,
need some help picking
the last of the Golden Delicious."
She nods, barely looks up
from the stool where she sits reading.
The broom balancing beside her
and the book in her hands
a clear signal
she'd still rather be in school
than sentenced to work.
Especially with me.

The rest of the crew has the tractor and trailer
a couple miles deep into the trees,
so we throw a few crates and a couple of picking sacks
in the back of Mr. D's truck
and bounce down the orchard path
to a section of young trees.
Color-picked earlier in the season,
only the stragglers remain.

The sun is out,
but it's cool enough
that goose bumps parade my arms
until the work warms me.
Mr. D glances my way, deciding
how to break the silence.
"How about your folks?
You hear much from them?"

I speak deliberately, translating
midthought as I tell him about Mutti's letters,
how I get *eins*—one—
maybe *zwei*—two—
a month.
Tell him I have three younger sisters
and send home most of my *Gehaltsscheck*
(rubbing my fingers together to sign the word for *money*)
with hope that they find food.
"What about your dad?" Mr. D asks.

"*Gestorben*.
Dead."
I speak quickly.
"*Diphtherie*—diphtheria.
I was *zwölf*, twelve."

"Twelve?" He sighs heavily,
in a way that signals his sympathy,
but then makes no attempt to comfort me
with simple platitudes,
doesn't try to fill the space
with words that won't make either of us feel better.

Instead he offers us both the grace of silence
as we reach into the trees.
I lift and twist,
do my best to pick the way he taught us
our first day,
forcing the stem
to separate from the spur
so that next year's apple isn't sacrificed
for this year's fruit.

Claire

TRUANT

●————————●

The shadows of late afternoon
have fallen,
and I'm alone with a book
in the salesroom
when Miss VerWys stops by
for apples.

Wisps of brown hair have fallen out from her bun
and she hugs her arms tight against her,
shivering at the October chill.
She picks out a peck of Jonathans,
then tells me I'm missed
in the schoolhouse.
That things aren't the same
without me.

She pauses and glances toward the house,
asks how my mom is faring.

I shrug,
unsure how to explain
the hollowness in my mom's eyes,
how slowly she moves
from her bedroom, to the table, and then back to bed.
Unsure how to explain

that while I share my mother's grief,
I'm angered by it too.
How I feel forced to swallow the bitterness
of losing not just my brother,
but the mother I used to have
and my own dreams as well.

But something about the understanding
in my teacher's eyes
tells me she doesn't really need an answer.
Tells me she's not here for the apples,
but to check up on me,
as a reminder
that she's not giving up on me.

And maybe I shouldn't either.

"My mom isn't well," I say,
"but things here should slow down
next month. Most apples will be sold
or hauled away by Thanksgiving."

And though it's almost unheard of
for a girl like me,
a girl who is needed at home,
a girl who is assumed to have all the education
she'd ever want
or need,
I dare suggest that maybe
I haven't quit school,
but only paused.

"I'd like to come back to school," I whisper.

"Oh, Claire, I'd like that too." She grips my shoulder.
"We'll find a way to catch you up.
This is a hard season,
but you've got so much ahead of you."

She releases her grip on me,
picks up her apples,
but as she turns toward the door, she turns again
and looks me directly in the eyes.
"I refuse to let your potential
go to waste."

I want to respond.
Want to thank her.
Want to believe her.
Instead, I just nod
and allow myself to be warmed
by her spark of hope.

Karl

BITTEN: BEGGING

Mr. D doesn't speak again
until we've filled another picking sack.
Until we are unhooking the ropes
of the fabric bottoms
to allow the yellow apples to tumble
softly into wooden crates.

"Crazy how mixed-up we all are.
Sent my own boy overseas,
traded him for German boys
working in my orchard.
He's not coming back,
and you don't have a pa
to go home to neither."

He heads back to the trees.
I follow,
choose the one next to him,
close enough to hear.
Pull back branches to dig deeper into the tree,
searching for fruit missed the first time through.

"You'd think I'd be used to it now,
the idea that nothing is really in my control.

That's the first lesson you learn
when you start farming.
You go through your days
whispering prayers.
For the last spring frost to come before
the first apple blossoms.
For the winds and hail of summer storms
to go north or south.
For the rain to come when you need it,
enough to water the land
but not flood it.
Though if the hail misses us,
it'll get someone else.
And if the rain comes,
I might battle blight.
There's a war on
and here I sit,
begging God to make nature behave.
Talking to the same God
who's listening to the prayers of mothers
asking that their sons come home,
boys asking that their planes aren't shot down.
And men
on both sides praying
that the enemy's bullets miss them."

I don't say anything,
just let him talk.
The dimming light of the waning afternoon
seems to open him up,
and any words I say now
could ruin the trance.

"I keep thinking of a refrain
I overhear the little kids singing in Sunday school,
about God having the whole world in his hands.
But when that whole world is needing help,
that whole world is hurting,
I wouldn't blame God if he doesn't have enough
attention to spend his time looking over here
at this slice of land.
Maybe it was selfish,
all those prayers for apples.
My son is dead
and we're here taking fruit out of trees,
apples I prayed would survive.
I want to be a man of faith,
but sometimes I wonder
if there isn't enough
God to go around."

Claire

WHAT IS RETURNED

●━━━━━━●

MONDAY, OCTOBER 23, 1944

The mailman,
who once smiled and waved every time he came by,
delivers a package.

The return address:
Army Effects Bureau in Kansas City.
Inside:
Whatever was found on Danny's dead body.
Whatever he carried with him.

Mama doesn't speak. Sets each item one by one on the
kitchen table.
A money order for $12.53.
His army jacket, folded and clean.
Nine letters Mama wrote,
two letters from me.
A worn picture of our family, taken May 1942.
We stand, smiling under the apple blossoms, dressed for
church.
I squint in the sun. I am eleven.
His dog tags, imprinted with his name, rank, and military
number.
A Petoskey stone,
found up north, on the shores of Lake Michigan
when he was eight,

carried in his pocket until it was rubbed smooth.
One letter intended for us, never finished.

> Dear Mom, Dad, and Claire (and Josie too, if she's
> reading these),
>
> It was good to hear my name at roll call today and get
> your letter, Mom. You sent it more than a month ago,
> but since it's September now, I can almost see you all
> there. Claire is back in school with her nose in a book,
> and Dad, you're outside dawn to dusk managing the
> crop, and Ma, you're keeping things running. It's strange
> to be in another world and to think of the apple season
> moving on without me, to know exactly what I'd be
> doing if I were home. I'd never craved an apple in my
> entire life—always had more than enough—but I have
> to say, grabbing one straight off a tree right now sounds
> darn good. Eat a few for me. The weather is mild here,
> and if I wasn't in a war, I might enjoy the scenery

My hands shake as I hold the letter,
and try to hear Danny's voice
in my head.
But it's already faint,
far away.

The reality that I'll never see him,
hear him,
hug him,
be teased by him,
grow up with him,

sucks all the air from my lungs.
Makes me wonder if I'll ever
breathe easily again.

Karl
LIEBE MUTTI: DEAR MOTHER

●————————————●

MONDAY, OCTOBER 23, 1944

The camp allows me to send home
one V-mail letter
(no more than twenty-four lines)
per week.

It's hard to know
how to fill even two dozen lines.
Do I tell my mother and sisters
that I'm well-fed
while they can barely find food
to put on their table?
Do I tell them that on Friday nights,
we watch Hollywood movies
on war surplus projectors
while they stare at the wall
or reread the same books,
the ones the Nazis haven't burned?
Do I tell them that I pick apples
in peace and sunshine,
while soldiers shout and march
past their door?

Do I tell them that the Americans
we've been told to hate
are becoming my friends,

and that the Nazis
we've been trained to obey
are who I now distrust?
Do I tell them about the connection I have
with the farmer's daughter;
that like me,
she is quiet and serious,
guarded but genuine.
How we both shoulder
the familiar weight of grief?

Mutti's letters to me
are short, vague,
arrive sporadically.
They come with words blacked out
or entire paragraphs cut by scissors,
proof that even my mother's words
must be inspected
by someone else's eyes
and hands
before I can earn them.
The words that are left
say that she loves me,
she misses me,
she worries.
The missing pieces
are clues
that make me return her worry.
Left to wonder
how many of her words
are stuck
in bags or boxes
between us.

I write about the weather,
how peaceful it is here
picking apples in the trees,
but cross my words out,
cautious to appear too content.
I write that the Americans
we work for are kind and decent,
but think better of it,
afraid to give too many clues
that my bitterness
has dissolved
along with my allegiance
to Hitler.

I set my pen down.

Censorship happens
on both sides of the ocean.

Claire

CAUGHT

Daddy's hauling apples across town
and Karl and I are watching customers.
We're low on cider.
"I'll go fill some jugs," I offer,
not minding a break from customers,
their questions and small talk.

When I open the wooden door of the cider house,
Ernst is there, broom in hand, smirking
like he has been expecting me.
"*Hallo!*"

My heart races
and I remind myself to breathe,
to keep the fear that bubbles up in my gut
out of my eyes.
My body screams of danger,
but my mind assures me I can handle myself.
My ego tells me to prove
I'm not afraid.

"I'm just grabbing some cider."
I start toward the holding tank.
Move confidently,
stand tall.

Avoid his eyes.
It's when I bend over to grab a cider jug
that I feel him
too close.
His breath on my neck.

I do not need to understand German
to know his whisper is threatening.
"Wo ist dein Schoßhund, Karl?"
His hand grips my shoulder
and I shiver at its weight,
the too-tight squeeze
of his cold fingers.

Maybe it would be smarter
to keep my mouth shut,
or to run immediately toward the door,
but I'm tired of backing down
from anything
or anyone
who threatens me.

Fear and adrenaline
boil up a boldness and bravery
I didn't know I had.

I pull out of his grasp and mutter,
"You don't belong here, Ernst,
in this country
or on this farm."

I convince myself to look up,
to look into the eyes of my enemy

long enough to see
his eyes have turned
from cocky amusement
to wild anger.
Long enough to realize
his hand
is no longer grasping
for my shoulder but coming
straight toward my face.

Karl

FALSCH: AMISS

●━━━━━━━━━━●

After delivering a half bushel
of Northern Spies
to an old man's back seat
("Careful now, don't bruise them."),
I watch his silver Buick pull out of the drive
and then glance over to the cider house
where Claire went to fill some jugs.

The windows are dirty and foggy,
but I catch
the reflection of a man,
someone much larger than Claire,
standing very close to her.

Mr. D's truck is gone.
Pete is working on a tractor in the barn.
I can't think of anyone else who should
be in the cider house alone with Claire.

I've never abandoned my post,
but my gut tells me
this is the time
to follow my instincts
rather than the rules;
that I'd rather risk

leaving the salesroom
long enough to investigate
who is in the cider house with Claire
than kick myself later
for once again
blindly following orders.

Claire

FIGHTING BACK

●━━━━━━━━━━●

My face stings
with the power of Ernst's palm,
and I reel back into a corner,
my mind too fuzzy to devise
an escape route.

Ernst is smiling now.
He steps closer again,
and I know he's the kind of man
who holds tightly to his Nazi training.
The kind of man who feels stronger
when he can make someone else feel scared.

I'm shaking,
but determined
to fight back.
I take a deep breath,
grip tight to the full, glass cider jug,
and raise it high,
aiming for his head.

My arms are already coming down
with the weight of the jug
when Karl throws open the door,
lunges for Ernst.

Karl has Ernst around the chest
just as my glass weapon comes down.
Ernst hits the concrete floor;
the jug clashes with Karl's forehead,
then bounces to the ground,
shatters,
spraying syrupy liquid,
sending glass shards flying.

I'm not even aware of my scream
as I watch them both go down,
wincing and rolling on the dirt floor,
sopping in cider
and decorated in glass splinters.

Blood trickles down Karl's face.
His head the victim
of my defense.

Karl
SCHLACHTFELD: BATTLEFIELD

●━━━━━━━━━●

WEDNESDAY, OCTOBER 25, 1944

Pete, hearing the commotion,
comes running from the barn
to find
a tangle of bodies,
cider,
blood,
curses.
Mr. D is close behind.

Pete drags Ernst up,
Mr. D grabs a rag
and pushes it to my head.
He leans over to
sit me up.

I look up to find Claire.
She stands
next to the cider tank,
hands covering her mouth,
shaking
but not bleeding.

She sputters
the few words needed to explain.
"He . . ." She points at Ernst,

still looks him in the eyes.
"Hit me.
Karl came in,
grabbed him as I . . ."
She pantomimes in slow motion
the smashing of the glass jug.

Mr. D leaves me to tend to myself
and walks slowly,
deliberately toward Ernst.

When Mr. D is close enough
to stare Ernst square in the eyes,
he throws a hard punch.
Finishes the job.

Claire

SEWING

Karl sits at our kitchen table.
I will my hands to stop shaking
long enough to thread a sterilized needle.

Daddy and Pete
are cleaning up the cider room,
and even Mama came out of the house
long enough to realize
she needed to keep the customers
distracted and happy.
Ernst sits outside,
holding his head in his hands
and dripping wet from getting sprayed down with the hose.
Nelson enjoyed the chance to cool him off,
and now has his eyes glued on him,
suddenly serious about his guard duties.

The gaping cut on Karl's forehead
refuses to quit bleeding,
begs for attention.

I first tried pressing a clean cloth to the jagged cut
that stretches from his eyebrow to his hairline.
But as soon as I removed the pressure,

the blood began again.
"I think our best bet
is a few stitches," I told him.
"A bandage isn't going to do the job."

If I want to be a nurse,
today is as good as any
to give it a try.

I take a deep breath
and pinch the thin skin together,
lean over him
to attempt my first stitch.
The needle goes into the loose skin easily.
He tries not to flinch.

I steady my hand and
steady my nerves.
Attempt to lighten the conversation.
"You just wanted to see
if I knew how to sew,
didn't you?"

He knows better
than to talk while I've got a needle in his head,
but when I glance down at his face,
his mouth is turned up in a grin.

Between us,
the space is small
and the silence thick.
I stay focused on my sewing.

But as I work, my mind buzzes:
Karl and I have barely talked since Danny's funeral,
but today, he may have earned
a second chance.
I shiver to think
what might have happened
had he not barged into the cider house
when he did.
If he hadn't chosen bravery
over allegiance
to his comrade.

"I guess I should say I'm sorry
for hitting you over the head
with a glass jug,"
I begin.

Still unsure how honest to be.
Still unsure how to thank him.
Still unsure I want to surrender my trust.

I use my wit to divert
from the weight of the moment:
"But if you would have let me save myself,
you wouldn't be in this mess."

Smiling, I gently tie off the thread,
back away to inspect my work.
Karl winces and touches his forehead.
The stitches are a bit sloppy,
but the bleeding has stopped.
The gap is closed.

"Thank you," he says,
and then he steers me back to reality.
"Are you okay, Claire?"

At the question,
at the genuine concern in his voice,
at his caring nod toward my throbbing cheek,
I realize that maybe I'm not.

I bite my lip,
push away the tears
that threaten to fill my eyes,
and nod.

Karl waits an extra beat,
gives me a chance
to tell the truth
before bracing himself to stand.
Clearly dizzy, he lowers himself back down,
pauses again,
gathering his balance
and his thoughts.
"Well, I guess I'm the one
who needed saving then,
aren't I?"

Karl

SCHMERZ: ACHE

●━━━━━━●

The sun is setting
as the truck takes our crew back to camp.
My head pounds,
a fresh jolt of pain pummels me
with every bump in the road.

The rumble of the truck's engine
allows me the anonymity
to be heard only by Otto,
who is squeezed in next to me.
I fill him in:
How I found Ernst cornering Claire,
how I lunged for him
just as she attacked with the cider jug.
How Claire stitched me up,
was all business,
a professional nurse.

What I don't tell him
is that what means more to me
than having my head patched up
is the hope
that Claire and I may have patched
up our friendship.
That I may have proven

I'm not like Ernst,
that I'm worth talking to again,
worth trusting.

Ernst has earned himself a spot
up in front, nestled tightly
between Pete and Nelson.
His legs straddle the truck's gear shifter
and his eyes stay on the road.
Nelson even threatened to find the handcuffs
he misplaced months ago.
Anton and Heinz sit on the opposite corner
of the truck bed, quiet and sullen
for the first time in months.

When Otto hears I plan to visit
the commander's office
as soon as we arrive back at camp,
he offers to come along,
provide me with backup
and confirm my story.

I tell him this is a trip
I need to make alone.

Claire

STORED UP

━━━━━●━━━━━●━━━━━

I wander back out to the salesroom
after Karl's stitches are done.
Mama looks up from the ledger book,
pauses,
and then runs to reach for me.
It's the first time I've felt her arms tight around me
in months,
maybe years.

She apologizes,
tells me she's sorry that when Danny died
her grief left no room for me.
Tells me she's sorry
for locking herself away
instead of figuring out how to hurt
alongside me.

Somehow, as I've grown older,
she's gotten so used to the idea
of my independence
that she stopped thinking
I still need to be held
now and then.

Months and months of stored-up sobs
find their way out of my body.
My shoulders shake.
I can't catch my breath.

We stand there for a long time.
No more words,
only weeping
witnessed by apples
picked by enemy hands.

Karl

WASCHLAPPEN: COWARD

Literal meaning: *dishrag*

—————•—————

WEDNESDAY, OCTOBER 25, 1944

Without worrying
about what a good German would do,
without thinking
about how Anton and Heinz
will make me pay later,
I march straight
to the camp's administration office
and knock on the commander's door.

I tell him everything.
That Ernst
is a Nazi,
a liar,
a criminal,
a danger.
I tell him what Ernst did to Claire.

He takes notes,
nods,
asks questions:
Did you see Ernst hit the girl?
Why was Ernst near her?
Why were you?

He stops to stare at my stitches,
the throbbing red
under my eye that is already
shading black and blue.

His questions satisfied,
I am dismissed.

I open the office door,
and there stand Nelson and Ernst
against the wall,
waiting and listening.
They must have followed just behind me.
I look Ernst in the eyes
as he tosses a German curse
upon me one last time:
"*Der Waschlappen.*"

I give him a mocking salute.

And walk away.

Claire

UNSAID

I can hear steady rain on the roof
when Daddy pops his head into my room.
It's early enough that it's still dark.
In a hushed voice, he tells me
it's supposed to be wet all day
and the market will be slow.
He's called off the POWs,
and I can sleep in too.

He tells me to go ahead and turn over,
fall back to sleep,
then lingers in my doorway,
adds, "Claire, Ernst won't be allowed back here.
You won't ever see
that boy again."

I nod and hope he might keep talking,
that he might also say
he's glad I'm okay,
he's sorry he didn't protect me,
he loves me.
But I guess those are words
I'm supposed to figure out on my own
or read in his eyes,

because he just stands there,
watching me.

Then I hear the familiar rhythm of his feet
headed down the stairs
and out to the orchard.

Karl

DER RUHETAG: DAY OF REST

—————•—————

I won't say aloud how badly
my head is smarting
or how glad I am for today's rain
that called us off work.

The commander made an announcement
at this morning's breakfast:
"Violent incorrigibles will not be tolerated.
Because Ernst Bernock maintains his allegiance
to the Nazi party
and has been deemed a danger
to civilians and POWs alike,
he will be transferred to a maximum-security
camp in Alva, Oklahoma."

Back in the barracks,
we debrief.
"I heard they call it Devil's Island,"
Anton says. His eyes are worried,
but softer. Like he's not quite sure
who he is
without Ernst,
without a bully to follow.

When there's little left to say,
most of the men wander out,
head to the rec room to play cards.
"You coming?" Otto asks.

"Nein. Gib mir eine Minute,"
I tell him, collapsing onto my bunk.

I think of Ernst traveling west.
Another stop on his journey.
Wonder if he still thinks his allegiance
is worth it.

I expected *Rache*—vengeance or justice
or whatever they call it when enough wrongs
finally make a right—
but my head feels as gray and watery
as the dark day outside.

Claire

TRANSFER

———•———

Yesterday's storms
earned the Germans a day off,
but all the commotion
stirred Mama enough
that she's ventured out
to work beside me
in the salesroom this morning.

"I've been thinking," she says.
"Things will be slowing down here,
and I can do my part.
Claire, you stepped in when we most needed you,
but now I know
your plans are bigger than this orchard."

Mama's eyes mist up and I almost think
she might grab me, hold me tight again.

But a customer comes into the driveway,
and she takes a deep, collecting breath.
"Help me for today,
and on Monday,
you get yourself back
to school."

As she turns away, I grab her arm.
"Mama,
thank you."

She smooths my hair,
tucks a loose flyaway
back behind my ear,
and turns to work.

Karl

APFELKUCHEN: APPLE PIE

●————————●

FRIDAY, OCTOBER 27, 1944

The ground is still wet,
so we eat lunch
on the picnic table and front stoop
of the DeBoer house:
Claire, Mr. D, Pete,
Nelson, and the nine of us.
When our sack lunches are gone,
Mrs. D comes out with a warm apple pie
and we all cheer.

She cuts and drops slices onto
small, white plates,
then heads into the house
to grab forks so we can eat it properly.
But before she's back,
we pick up the pie with our hands
and devour it with barely a breath,
lick the gooey warm apples
straight off our fingers.

Claire seems relaxed,
and I realize this is the most
I've seen her smile
since her brother died.
She takes the end of the wooden bench—

next to Pete, across from me—
still keeping a safe distance
from the rest of the men.
"I'm going back to school on Monday," she announces.
"You fellas are just going to have to find a way
to manage around here without me."

Pete gently elbows her,
smiling wide.
"Good for you, girl.
You got too many brains to be hanging
around here with us jugheads anyway."

"*Das ist gut*, Claire," I say,
forgetting to translate.
She glances at my forehead,
nods at her crooked stitches on display.
"Healing," I say.
"*Danke*, Nurse DeBoer."

She smiles,
not in spite of me,
but at me.
"Now you'll have a scar
to remember me by," she says.

I nod,
touch the sticky skin
that's already doing its best to heal up.
Imagine the scar I'll always carry.
Know I'll always be able to touch my head
and remember
Claire's stitches,

that I was able to display some courage
when it counted,
and spent time at this apple orchard
in a place called Michigan.

Claire

BACK TO SCHOOL

●━━━━━━━━●

MONDAY, OCTOBER 30, 1944

It's chilly enough
that I've pulled on my wool stockings
under my long skirt
for my first day back
to school.
I'm glad to be back,
but feel years older
than when I last entered this schoolyard.
My stomach churns at the memory
of running this trail,
that moment when Pete came to get me
to let me know
my life had changed forever.

When they see me coming, the little kids cheer,
and kindergartner Gertie
runs over and squeezes my waist.
She peers up at me,
and when I ooh and ahh over her newly lost front tooth,
she grins brighter.
"I've been waiting for you, Claire," she says,
and then squeezes me a little tighter
before running off.

I don't dillydally in the yard like the others,
but head straight up the steps
before Miss VerWys is at the door with her bell.
She's working at her desk.
When she glances up,
she rushes toward me.
I almost think she might hug me like Gertie,
but she squeezes my hands instead.
"I'm so glad to see you, Claire."

I don't complain today
when I'm assigned as a tutor for the little ones
for a good part of the morning.
And when Miss VerWys calls me to her desk,
she whispers that she knew I'd be back,
and pulls out some high school math and science
books I can dig into.
My heart soars and I nearly have to wipe tears
from my eyes.

She puts the books into my hands and says,
"I promise I'll do my best
to get you ready for whatever's next."

Karl
ZERRISSEN: TORN

The salesroom is slow today,
so I'm with the rest of the crew,
picking the late bloomers,
the Northern Spies.
They're a hard, crisp apple,
and when I sample one
straight off a tree,
the bitter tart mixes
with the cold morning air
and I shiver.

Mrs. D is handling the salesroom by herself.
I imagine Claire back at the schoolhouse.
I wonder when I might see her,
talk with her again.

And what comes next for us?
When the apples are all picked
and sold or shipped away,
where will they send us?
Maybe a factory or cannery
like some of the others at camp,
the unlucky ones
who haven't been assigned a job outside,

who haven't spent their days
in the sanctuary of silent trees.

Bits and pieces
of news from Germany
trickle over here.
From the sound of it,
we are losing.
My head is a tangle of thoughts,
not even sure who *we* are anymore
or how clean, simple words
like *gewinnen und verlieren*—
winning and losing—
could possibly be used to describe war.
As if it's a game,
rather than brutal bloodshed.

Otto picks next to me.
His letters from home
have only contained heartbreak:
two brothers dead, his dad paralyzed,
his parents moved in with an aunt.

Sick of serious talk,
we toss around fantasies like apples.
If they were to set us free
to explore this country,
where would we go first?
"West to the mountains," Otto says,
"and then south to warm beaches
with palm trees waving."

"I think I'd find a train,"
I say, "head north
to the Canadian wilderness.
Find a boat and fish."

What I don't say out loud
is that I also imagine
Claire beside me,
leaning easily into me
as we watch
the miles go by.

I dream.
I escape.

Claire

SAFE AND WARM

●————————————●

The kids at school were restless and rowdy
all day, jabbering about Halloween,
dressing up, and trick-or-treating.

I change into my farm clothes
as soon as I get home.
Mama is making dinner, so I offer to finish up
in the salesroom,
tidy up, restock,
help the last customers of the night.

As I approach the salesroom,
Karl is also heading the same way,
his arms flexing under the weight
of a crate of Winesaps.
I rush ahead to grab the door for him
and his smile widens as he sees me.

I shut the door behind us,
keep out the cold wind of October's final day.

Karl shivers as he sets down the crate
then walks toward me,
back toward the door,
but stops just short,

beside me.
My heart beats out of my chest
to have him here,
alone,
that smile so close.

"Miss having you around here, Claire," he says
as he blows into his cold hands.
I reach out to warm
his cold fingers with mine.
At our touch,
electricity surges through me
and I'm aware of what I've done.

I let out half a giggle
and let go of Karl's hands.
But he stays put,
doesn't rush to move away,
picks my hands up again,
squeezes them gently.

The warmth in his touch
is an assurance
that he is safe.
His face now serious,
but full of gratitude
for even this small gift of grace.

The salesroom door suddenly opens
and Karl and I jump away
from each other.
Pete walks in
and looks at Karl.

"I just told the other fellas
it's time to start loading up," he says.
"They're all wound up,
excited for their Halloween party
at the camp tonight."

Then he turns to me.
"Going trick-or-treating, sweetie?" Pete asks.
I shake my head.

"Too old for that stuff, Pete."

He glances over at Karl,
then me again.
"How about you ride along tonight, then?
You can keep me company,
help me keep these boys in line."

I shrug and nod,
then glance behind me,
share a secret smile with Karl
as we follow Pete to the truck.

Karl

TAGESENDE: DAY'S END

I watch Claire climb into the front seat,
wait for her to turn
her head as I join the others
in the truck bed behind her.
When she does,
I wink.
I'm going have to hide my smile before
the rest of the men start asking questions.

The gray afternoon
has given way to dimming light.
If the sun ever rose today,
we never glimpsed it.

The truck rumbles down the road
while my stomach still flutters.
"What going on?"
Otto elbows and asks me,
but we're interrupted by Pete,
who hollers out the window
to keep an eye out for children in costumes
making their way to the town hall.

And sure enough,
all along the side of the road, we see

a girl draped in the white cloth of a makeshift ghost,
a boy dressed in a baseball uniform
with *Detroit* scrawled across his chest,
another pretending to be a little soldier.
He wears camouflage pants tucked into his boots,
an old, oversized suit jacket,
and proudly balances a BB gun on his shoulder.
A helmet wobbles on his head as he marches.

Wilhelm offers the first notes of a song,
and as if we're part of a parade,
and as we've done on so many other drives back to camp,
we all join in and belt it out together.

Caught up in the revelry,
the chains of war
fall off our chests,
and our voices loosen,
the melody carrying us away.

I feel light tonight
as our voices blend in the wind
and echo off each other,
traveling down the road,
dissipating into the surrounding fields
like a low fog.

Abend wird es wieder	Eventide falls again
Über Wald und Feld	over woods and fields
Säuselt Frieden nieder	Peace is whispering down
und es ruht die Welt.	and the world is at rest.

The words linger in my head,
and I realize
this is the closest I've felt to peace,
to happiness,
in months.

Claire

RIDING SHOTGUN

●━━━━━━━●

TUESDAY, OCTOBER 31, 1944

We're bouncing down the road,
the men are singing loudly,
and I smile,
straining to hear Karl's voice
among the chorus.
We're almost crossing the railroad tracks
just out of town
when Pete and I grin at each other,
then crane our necks
to glimpse
the concert
coming from behind us.

All at once, a low roar,
like a tornado or a jet engine,
drowns out their voices.
We jerk our heads back around
toward the driver's side window
just in time to see a black beast barreling
straight at us.

I grab Pete's shoulder
as his foot pounds the gas pedal,
attempting to launch us
out of danger's reach.

My scream is drowned out
by a train's panicked squeal
as two thousand tons of weight
crunch
against the flimsy metal of our back end,
the bed where we carry our men.

As if struck by lightning,
the truck jolts,
my head thrashes
into the dash,
and we're spinning.
    spinning,
        spinning,
            spinning.
                My world goes black.

MICHIGAN WRECK ENDS
LIFE FOR TEN PERSONS

MIDWEST GAZETTE   November 1, 1944

Nine German prisoners of war and one American soldier, Nelson Johnson of Cadillac, Michigan, who was serving as their guard, were fatally injured when a train collided with their truck at a train crossing yesterday.

The civilian driver and a 13-year-old female passenger survived and are reported in serious condition.

A New York Central train demolished the truck, striking it broadside, displacing the men and strewing wreckage 300 feet. The men, who were riding in the bed of the truck, were returning to the POW Camp Lakewood in Allegan after work in a local orchard.

A funeral service for the German soldiers will be held at Fort Custer National Cemetery on Wednesday, Nov. 8.

German prisoners killed:

Friedrich Acker   Wilhelm Müller
Otto Arzberger   Heinz Schaefer
August Brandt   Walter Schmidt
Karl Hartmann   Norbert Weber
Anton Mayer

Claire

SOMEHOW ALIVE

———•———

WEDNESDAY, NOVEMBER 1, 1944

Danny's dead body is somewhere
in Europe,
while thirty miles down the road,
at the National Cemetery,
they will plant nine German bodies
in the ground.

They will bury Karl.

I think of his hands,
his smile.
The careful way his voice,
his accent,
curled around my name.

And I lie in a hospital bed.
Somehow alive.
Mama sleeps in a chair beside me.

My head pounds and protests
and I want to go back to sleep.
Avoid the pain
of my body
and my mind.
Of my memories.

Bile rises in my throat
when my mind flashes to Ernst.
The one who is expelled and banished,
but alive and well
in a camp where he serves another sentence
that earned him
his life.
The only soldier to live
is the one who never let go of Hitler's orders,
the one who never admitted his guilt,
the one whose heart was never loosened
from the teachings that wound it tight with hate.

My body throbs.
I ache down to the marrow of my bones.
But the worst pain is my heart,
bashed and battered,
aware that each time
its gaping wounds
seem to get haphazardly stitched
back together,
this war
finds a way to tear it wide open
again.

Karl

AUF WIEDERSEHEN ZU MEINER MUTTER: HOW I SAID GOODBYE TO MY MOTHER

———————•

Claire

WHIPLASHED

●━━━━━━━━●

FRIDAY, NOVEMBER 3, 1944

The pink of sunrise seeps through the window
of my hospital room, cold frost clouding
the glass's edge.
My mind wrestles with time.
Is this the third morning
I've woken in this room?

I'm uncertain if I prefer the stark bright
of reality or the fog
in which I've been floating.
When I attempt to sit up,
pain washes over me.
Every piece of my insides
shaken up and screaming.

Mama and Daddy assure me they slept
in their own beds last night,
but they're back here already,
begging me to eat the oatmeal
that has been delivered.
My right arm sits heavy
against my chest, wrapped tightly in a cast.

During a morning check,
the nurse suggests I should try a walk.

Yesterday's X-rays revealed my legs are whole,
but when I try to swing them out of bed
to stand, I'm not sure they'll hold.
My parents each take an arm and guide me
down the bright white of the hospital hallway.
We move slowly, and I can't help
but peer into each of hospital's empty rooms,
each empty bed a reminder
of the dead POWs who don't need one,
whose bodies are being prepared for burial
rather than being fixed.

My mind flashes to those last moments,
his hands in mine,
our secret smile,
the wink as he climbed into the truck behind me,
the joy on his face
as he joined his comrades
and sent his voice into the night air.

I'm not sure what the smallest measure of time is called,
but I know it was how fast my laughter
transformed to terror
when I turned to see that train.
My parents thought I was sleeping last night
when they discussed the men's bodies being flung,
some hundreds of feet
by the impact of the collision.

I stop when I realize we are passing Pete's room.
He is sitting up in bed,
bandaged and staring vacantly ahead.
My parents' eyes try to tell me no,

that this will be too hard,
but I pull them through the doorway.
"Claire wants to say hello, Pete," my dad says
in a voice so chipper it's jarring.
When Pete looks over at me,
he bites hard on his lip and his eyes tear up.
At his bedside, I reach for his hand
with my good one.

"I'm sorry, Claire," he says.
"I didn't see . . ."
My parents rush to give assurances
and explanations
about bad conditions,
tall weeds,
trees obstructing the view.
I squeeze Pete's hand,
knowing that the word *accident* is too small,
doesn't hold the power
to treat an ounce of the pain
that sits heavily on his chest.

"We better get you back to your room
and let Pete rest," my mom says,
prodding me away, pretending
peace can be secured that simply.

Karl

AUF WIEDERSEHEN ZU MEINEN SCHWESTERN: HOW I SAID GOODBYE TO MY SISTERS

———————•

Claire

STUBBORN

———————•———

On the drive home from the hospital,
Daddy tries to talk me out of coming along
to Wednesday's funeral,
says it will all be men from the camp,
says I won't be up for it,
says it will be too hard for me.

I tell him I will be dressed and ready.
I tell him that I am coming with him.
I tell him that if I worked beside them,
I will see them buried.
I'm old enough to decide
for myself
where I belong.

He doesn't take his eyes off the road, but nods.

Mama, in the passenger seat,
sits silently.
Her face to the window,
still brittle
with grief.
There is no question of her coming along.
We all know that watching more boys—

anyone's boys—
lowered into their graves
will break her
for good.

Karl

AUF WIEDERSEHEN ZU CLAIRE: HOW I SAID GOODBYE TO CLAIRE

———————•

Claire

FUNERAL AGAIN

With my arm slung in a cast,
it's an easy decision not to wear my funeral dress.
At this point, I'd prefer to burn it anyway.
It hangs heavy in my closet,
reminding me of everything and everyone
I'll never get back.

Daddy says nothing when I come into the kitchen
in a pair of black pants
and a white blouse that will be covered
by a heavy winter coat.
Mama—who helped me dress,
pulling the shirt gently over my bad arm,
buttoning my shirt
like she did when I was little girl—
is still in her nightdress,
gripping a cup of black coffee
by the door as we leave.
The sky spits cold today,
not quite snowflakes or rain,
but a bitter sleet that stings our faces.

The funeral is held at a wooden chapel
inside the national cemetery.

The preacher doesn't know these boys,
doesn't know me.

His sermon—
in English, of course—
means little to the bodies that lie in coffins,
draped with striped flags.
Means little to the other POWs,
the dozens of men from camp
who fill the pews,
work at other farms,
pick other people's fruit, sugar beets, beans.
The other men who didn't die in a bloody war,
who weren't assigned to a work group
that was hit by a train no one saw coming,
who might someday travel home.
I can't look at their faces.

If I do, I'll think of the stitches
I sewed on Karl's head,
his body in the box,
his wound not yet healed.
I'll think of how he'll never have the scar
I promised.
If I do, I'll think of Danny.
The sound of his laughter as he picked on a ladder
above me,
always making sure a few wayward apples
dropped on my head,
his quick kick under the table at dinner
when I was about to give away one of our secrets,
his stubborn refusal to back away from a challenge
when he believed what he was doing was right.

When the preacher stops talking,
a short POW with freshly combed hair,
his military uniform pressed,
moves to the front of the church,
holding a violin.
He stands amid the crowded coffins,
raises his instrument to his chin,
and plays "Ave Maria."
The rippling waves
of the song crack
me open,
and I drop
my head
and weep.

A PROCLAMATION TO THE AMERICAN PEOPLE

From Harry S. Truman

**Delivered from the Radio
Room at the White House**

May 8, 1945

The Allied armies, through sacrifice and devotion and with God's help, have wrung from Germany a final and unconditional surrender. The western world has been freed of the evil forces which for five years and longer have imprisoned the bodies and broken the lives of millions upon millions of free-born men. They have violated their churches, destroyed their homes, corrupted their children, and murdered their loved ones. Our Armies of Liberation have restored freedom to these suffering peoples, whose spirit and will the oppressors could never enslave . . .

Claire

BLOSSOMS

●————————————●

TUESDAY, MAY 8, 1945

School was canceled today
for what they're calling Victory Day.
At nine a.m., Mama, Daddy, and I gather around the radio
to listen to President Truman
announce that Germany has surrendered,
that America is set free from the evil forces
that have imprisoned our bodies
and broken our lives.

After the president's speech, newscasters lecture
about *winners,*
losers,
allies,
enemies.
The words seem to fall out of their mouths
so easily
while they get stuck in mine.
I have names for each of those words.
Faces that don't fit easily
within simple definitions.

Daddy takes a deep breath
and switches off the radio.
Like me,
his mind seems full,

but his voice is silent.
He squeezes my shoulder
and then kisses Mama on the cheek
before going back out to the barn.
Mama says she needs to start the wash,
but I'm free to study.

Instead, I sneak away
into the trees
alone.

The afternoon is quiet
and the ground is damp.
The robins have returned
and flutter tree to tree.
The spring breeze catches my attention,
its scent a combination
of decay and new life.

While cities celebrate with ticker-tape parades
and patriots cheer and wave
American flags from tall balconies,
I walk among the bloom
of delicate apple blossoms.
Consider that from these tender buds,
apples will grow.
Even while I understand
how quickly one bitter morning,
one late frost,
could kill them all.

I take a deep breath in.

And I hear them.
I see them.

I hear Danny telling me to stop and notice
the sweet smell that surrounds me.
I see him pulling down a branch to admire it,
reminding me
to stop and pay attention.
Reminding me not to miss
the good
that remains.

And I hear Karl,
his voice still heavy with regret,
but brave enough
to dare himself to do better.
He quietly prods me to consider
the idea of forgiveness,
the possibility of a fresh start.
His eyes, a medley of pain and wonder,
stare straight through me.
Ask me to consider
if hope could be found
on the other side of pain.

As their voices fade,
I draw in closer to the tree in front of me.
A stubborn root catches my foot,
and I press my sole upon it.
Visualize the web of roots
that spread out under me,
that plunge deep into the earth,

that hold this tree steady
through the winter, dark nights, storms.

I run my hand along its wrinkled trunk,
look up at the branches
dormant through the winter,
the green leaves that now sprout,
the shoots that aim toward the sky
with stubborn resilience.

And I have no doubt
that where I'm from,
what I've lived through,
is planted deep inside me—
that all my life,
I'll be drawn back here,
to the trees,
to the apples.

But I am also confident
that I am finding my own place on the branch,
a space to grow
where the sun will reach me.

AUTHOR'S NOTE

My grandfather managed an apple orchard for most of his life. I grew up calling it Grandpa's Orchard, though technically the two hundred acres of apples (plus fifty-some acres of peaches, cherries, and plums) never belonged to our family. My dad and his siblings were raised on that farm, and in many ways, I was too. It's hard to separate our family history from the acres of rolling land where we picked apples, took tractor rides perched on Grandpa's lap, built forts, and played with our cousins.

Several years ago while working on an essay for a college course, my dad mentioned to me a story he had once been told by the owners of the land: that during World War 2, a decade before Grandpa and his young family came to live on the farm, German prisoners had been hired to help pick that fall's crop of apples.

Fascinated by this tidbit of information, I began extensive research on the German POWs who were herded onto once-empty Victory ships returning from delivering supplies to Europe, a solution to the country's labor shortage. I learned that from 1943 to 1946, 425,000 POWs—mostly Germans, but some Italians—came to more than five hundred labor camps across the United States. In Michigan, where our family's orchard was located, thirty-two base camps housed prisoners plucked out of war and, in many ways, saved by being captured. Most were grateful to give up their guns, relieved to be sent to camps where they were well-fed and outsourced to farms that might give them the task of picking celery, apples, or sugar beets.

Though farmers and their families were warned not to

fraternize with the enemies that arrived on their land, those instructions were not heeded carefully. Enemy lines quickly began to blur when people talked and worked side by side. The prison guards who accompanied the POWs to farms— often GIs classified as unfit for combat—were by and large a laid-back crew and quick to turn their heads if the POWs were invited to the farmhouse for dinner, especially if they were invited to partake too. Though a few ardent Nazis pushed their weight around in the camps, many POWs slowly grew more wary of the German Nationalism diet they had been fed their entire lives, more distrustful of Hitler and the Nazi party after each day spent on American soil. Like Karl, near the end of the war many German soldiers were just teenagers, boys who were mandated to become members in the Hitler Youth and attended schools that included racial science and eugenics as part of their curriculum. Also like Karl, the painful and convicting process of disillusionment began for many German POWs the day they sailed into an American harbor and discovered that the country had not, as they were told, been bombed to ruins. Through conversations with Americans, newspapers and magazines made available to them in prison camps, and exposure to films, theater, and books once banned from their viewing, the lies and hatred their lives had been built upon crumbled much like their war-torn hometowns back in Germany.

Details on the POWs who worked inside my grandpa's orchard are fuzzy and few, but the story, as it was passed on to my dad, goes like this: as the fall sun crept down toward the horizon at the end of their final day during their last shift, the prisoners cried as they were told it was time to leave, because they were worried about now being killed by the Americans.

But something never felt right to me about this interpretation of the story, and I found myself doubting its simplicity and assumption. In many ways, the story of Claire and Karl became my pursuit to add depth, understanding, and complexity to the one piece of a very large puzzle I was given.

Claire and Karl's story is a work of fiction. They aren't real people, though their lives are based on my family history and stories I've read about the soldiers and families whose lives intersected on American soil while the war raged on in Europe. Most historical sources paint a fairly idyllic picture—not perfect, but not adversarial—of this American experiment of bringing the enemy home to do the work left behind while we sent soldiers to Europe. While I worked hard to maintain historical accuracy, I also hope readers will come to better understand the toll and complexity of war, as well as the dangers of nationalism and blind loyalty. My attempt is not to excuse or justify the horrors of the Holocaust or the evil that soldiers like Karl were wrapped up in, but to better understand it and prevent it from happening again. In portraying Karl's humanity, I hope it can be understood how German youth raised under Hitler's vile regime were used as his weapons, while also becoming his victims.

Claire's American home front experience is rooted in my family history as well. Neither my maternal nor paternal grandmother went to school past the eighth grade, as education was often seen as needless for women, who were assumed to have no career expectations beyond that as a mother and home-maker. Both of my grandfathers also dropped out of school after eighth grade, including the grandpa who eventually went on to manage the apple orchard. His father died when he was just a toddler, and his two brothers left to serve in World War 2 when he was about Claire's age, so he had no choice but to quit school and help his mom run the family farm.

The news articles included in this novel are adapted from real ones published in local papers (presented in the book as

coming from the fictional *Midwest Gazette*), the story on con-
centration camps that Karl and Otto discover is taken from
the actual September 11, 1944 issue of *TIME*, and the book
concludes with an excerpt from President Truman's V-E Day
announcement of German surrender. Other historical documents, such as the rules about interacting with prisoners and
the telegram, are also based on primary sources. I made every
attempt to make this story as accurate and realistic as possible,
including the POWs' journey to the US, their living conditions in the camps, and the tragic train accident at the end of
this story. (I've also provided these sources in the bibliography
section in the back so you can engage with them as well.)

On October 31, 1944, in Blissfield, Michigan, a group of
twenty-four POWs were riding in the back of a truck on their
way back to camp after a day harvesting sugar beets when
they were struck by a westbound New York Central passenger train. Sixteen of the POWs and their guard were instantly
killed, while the others were rushed to local hospitals. As my
poem details, it was Halloween night and the POWs were tired
from a long day of work, but excited for festivities planned at
the camp. Sources say the "low and dark" sky and tall trees
and weeds obstructed the driver's view, and that the vehicle
was dragged for more than forty feet while bodies were sent
flying three hundred feet from the point of impact. Though
I only included one funeral in my story, in actuality there
were three funerals held for the POWs—one Lutheran, one
Catholic, and one for the men listed as "non-religious." Fellow
prisoners served as the pallbearers and all were buried in Fort
Custer National Cemetery, along with ten other POWs who
died of various causes during their time in America.

In 2019, I was invited by historian Greg Sumner, whose
book *Michigan POW Camps in World War II* served as an
indispensable source for my novel, to visit the graves of

the POWs while attending a ceremony to commemorate *Volkstrauertag*—the German National Day of Mourning, which is held each year on the third Sunday in November at the national cemetery. More than just a Veteran's Day, *Volkstrauertag* remembers not only soldiers killed in wars, but anyone who died due to oppression because of race, religion, disability, or conviction.

I recruited my dad to join me on my research mission and was astounded when we pulled up to the cemetery to see a crowd of people gathered around the white tombstones of the POWs. We stood in the wind and the cold to listen to a program that included music from a Detroit-based German choir, the firing of shots from an honor guard, and a memorial address from Wolfgang Moessinger, the Consulate General of Chicago, who challenged the crowd not to forget "the people who had been abused by a criminal government at the time" and expressed his thankfulness for the American people willing to "look after these victims."

That's what I most hope to accomplish with these pages: to "look after" these characters who represent the real humans ravaged by war—the victims and the accomplices, the allies and the enemies, the vulnerable and the misled.

Though a work of fiction, this story is as real to me—and I hope for you too—as the apples that grow each fall on the new trees my parents have now planted. Like Claire and Karl, the fall of 1944 planted deep seeds within me: seeds of wonder, sorrow, regret, goodness, pain, and beauty. The roots of those emotions are now wound so tightly together that I couldn't separate one from another if I tried. My grandfather's apple trees are gone now, the old orchard bulldozed to make room for subdivisions, but deep underground, I know the tangled roots of history remain.

SOURCES

"250 German Prisoners of War to be Housed at Lakeview Camp," *Allegan News*, May 19, 1944. Accessed via Allegan District Library archives, https://www.alleganlibrary.org /local_history/digitized_newspapers.php.

Bartoletti, Susan Campbell. *Hitler Youth: Growing up in Hitler's Shadow*. New York: Scholastic Focus, 2019.

Carlson, Lewis H. *We Were Each Other's Prisoners: An Oral History of World War II American and German Prisoners of War*. New York: Basic Books, 1998.

"Foreign News: Murder, Inc." *TIME*. Time Inc., September 11, 1944. https://content.time.com/time/magazine/article /0,9171,775229,00.html.

Garcia, J. Malcolm. "German Pows on the American Homefront." Smithsonian.com. Smithsonian Institution, September 15, 2009. https://www.smithsonianmag.com /history/german-pows-on-the-american-homefront -141009996/.

Hall, Kevin T. "The Befriended Enemy: German Prisoners of War in Michigan." *Michigan Historical Review* 41, no. 1 (2015): 57. https://doi.org/10.5342/michhistrevi.41.1.0057.

"Michigan Wreck Ends Life for 17 Persons." *The Sandusky Register*, Nov. 1, 1945. Accessed via Newspapers.com, https://www.newspapers.com/paper/the-sandusky-register /228/.

Sumner, Gregory D. *Michigan POW Camps in World War II*. Charleston, SC: The History Press, 2018.

"Victory in Europe: Day of Prayer." Harry S. Truman. https://www.trumanlibrary.gov/library/proclamations /2651/victory-europe-day-prayer.

ACKNOWLEDGMENTS

I was raised inside a family of apple growers and story-tellers, and the landscapes where those stories were first told to me are embedded in this story. I'm especially grateful for my dad's stories and memories, especially that small tidbit he shared with me about the German POWs who came to pick apples on our orchard one fall during World War 2, and that my mom, the "Apple Lady," instilled in me the stubborn persistence and faith to tackle this project. To my siblings, cousins, aunts, and uncles, I hope you see in these pages reflections of our collective memories and trees that have tied us together.

This novel grew from a nonfiction essay that became a few experimental poems that became my thesis project while studying at the Naslund-Mann Graduate School of Writing at Spalding University. I'm grateful to my classmates and the staff at Spalding, led by Kathleen Driskell, and my mentors and workshop leaders: Nancy McCabe, Leah Henderson, Dianne Aprile, Edie Hemingway, Beth Bauman, and Silas House, and especially Lesléa Newman, who worked with me for multiple semesters before taking me on as a personal student. Lesléa's fingerprints are all over this novel, which she nurtured and believed in from its earliest drafts.

Greg Sumner and his book, *Michigan POW Camps in World War II*, were invaluable resources and guides. Greg's careful research and exploration of the stories and people behind the historical notes and documents left behind provided the backbone of this novel.

I am indebted to my friend Rory Callendar, who generously read an early draft and provided help with the integration of the German language. *Ich schulde dir noch ein Getränk.*

My agents, Amy Thrall Flynn and Rubin Pfeffer, were enthusiastic, supportive, insightful, and kind. I'm so glad for their generosity and guidance.

I knew I was in good hands from my first meeting with my editor, Katherine Easter, who is as kind and perceptive on the page as she is in person. I cherish her warmth, keen eye, attention to nuance, and desire to drive ever closer to the heart of this story. In addition, my copyeditor, Jacque Alberta, held all things together, including me. They—along with Sara Merritt, Jessica Westra, and the entire Zonderkidz team—have treated me and this story with great care.

To Team Perfect, my Book Club, my Small Group, and every friend, family member, and colleague who read early drafts, inquired about how things were going, sat with me through the waiting, and cheered with me when good news came: thank you. You have each sustained me.

I'm grateful that Jack Ridl taught me how to approach a poem and how to embrace the gifts of the perfectly imperfect. He continually reminds me to be with my readers, as he is always with me.

Elizabeth Felicetti, my "writing soulmate," checks in on me daily and helps me make my writing a priority. I am spoiled by her consistency, ruthless encouragement, and sharp humor.

Natalie Dykstra has been an unfaltering friend and mentor for decades, and it was under her care as an undergraduate that I first began my orchard research. Not for one second will I take her phone calls, wisdom, laughter, and enthusiasm for granted.

The students I was entrusted with and learned from over the years as a middle school teacher sat on my shoulder as I wrote these pages: my favorite part of teaching was match-making readers and books, and it's an honor to have this book join the beautiful chorus of voices on classroom and library bookshelves.

To my sons Caleb, Josh, and Levi, thank you for the space you've given me to get these words down and for providing enough humility, distraction, and joy to remember my center.

Tim, you are analytical and pragmatic in almost all things—except for your belief and support of me, in which you always go out on a limb. I am so grateful to have you always beside me. I love you.

Finally, to all who have taken the time to read this story, thank you. Frederik Buechner wrote: "My story is important not because it is mine, God knows, but because if I tell it anything like right, the chances are you will recognize that in many ways it is also yours. Maybe nothing is more than important than that we keep track, you and I, of these stories of who we are and where we have come from and the people we have met along the way, because it is precisely through these stories in all the particularity, as I have long believed and often said, that God makes himself known to each of us most powerfully and personally." And to that I echo: Amen.